GOD'S EYES

GOD'S EYES

GLENN DAVIS

TATE PUBLISHING
AND ENTERPRISES, LLC

Published by Tate Publishing & Enterprises, LLC
127 E. Trade Center Terrace | Mustang, Oklahoma 73064 USA
1.888.361.9473 | www.tatepublishing.com

Tate Publishing is committed to excellence in the publishing industry. The company reflects the philosophy established by the founders, based on Psalm 68:11,
"The Lord gave the word and great was the company of those who published it."

Book design copyright © 2014 by Tate Publishing, LLC. All rights reserved.
Cover design by Nikolai Purpura
Interior design by Raimie McDaniel

Published in the United States of America

ISBN: 978-1-62994-442-5
1. Biography & Autobiography / Personal Memoirs
2. Biography & Autobiography / General
14.02.01

In the beginning, we were all born somewhere. I was born in the hospital. It was the usual setting, and of course everything came out fine. At least you might think so. It was supposed to be a happy time, but it wasn't. After I was born, my mother was rolled back to her bed, and as you can imagine, she was worse for the wear. After a period of time, she came to. "Oh, where am I?"

The doctor sitting by her bed said, "You are at the Baker Hospital, and you are in Charleston, South Carolina. Do you understand me?"

My mother, who was groggy at the time, said, "My baby. I remember I was having a baby."

The doctor, who looked at her like he wished that she hadn't even mentioned it, said, "Yes ma'am, you did have a baby, and he was a beautiful, bouncing boy."

My mother, excited on hearing the news, asked, "Where is my baby?"

The doctor looked glum as he said, "The baby will stay here, but we had to contact social services. We know your problem. We know that you are an alcoholic."

The mother, who looked shocked, said, "Doctor, I can assure you that I'm not what you think."

The doctor, who was getting angry at this time, said "You see this is part of your problem. You don't realize that you have a problem, and it made me angry at you when that little fella came out and wouldn't you know it, it was deformed because of your drinking." The woman, who turned her face into her pillow, started weeping.

Well, there I am in the first row in the first cradle. I was in pretty bad shape, and it looked like there was no hope. And there was also concern that no one would be interested in a baby with so many health problems. The nurses were very nice to me and took care of me as if they were my mom. They were concerned about my feet because I was born with a clubfoot. The heel of my foot was where the toes should be. During one particular shift when the nurses had their attention on me, one of them said, "I know a friend of mine that would not at all mind adopting this little one."

The other nurse, looking skeptical, said, "Even with all these health problems? And it's not only that, he may even die."

The other looked at her like she should be slapped for doubting her faith, said, "Yes, even with all these health problems and the possibility that he could die; she is desperate to have this baby." The nurse at first thought she was crazy, then suddenly realized that it was the only hope that I had. She agreed that if she knew the lady's phone number, she ought to call it as soon as possible, and let her know the good news.

The nurse decided to call her friend and let her know that a beautiful baby boy was going to be in her future. When the phone rang on the other end, the woman was in the kitchen. As the phone rang, she had to run through an obstacle course but she finally made it to the phone. "Hello," she said, breathing loudly.

The nurse on the other end said, "Marge, are you there? Are you all right?" Marge, who had regained herself, said, "Yes, I guess so. I can't run to the phone like I used to when I was a kid."

The nurse, who laughed, said, "Well, I have some great news to tell you."

"What on earth do you mean?"

The nurse giggled. "I mean, silly, that you are having one of your dreams come true, right now as we are speaking."

Marge, getting a little frustrated, said, "What on earth are you talking about?"

The nurse said, "You remember the dream you told me about? You know, the one where if you couldn't have children, that you wanted to adopt?"

Marge's eyes were getting larger by the second, and she said, "You mean that you have a baby that Cecile and I can adopt?"

Karen, who was a long-time friend of Marge and who was very happy for her, said, "Yes, that dream is coming very true, and it is very possible that you and Cecile have a chance for it to come true. And, Marge, if you want that little precious life, you and Cecile had better get to the hospital right now and get the paper work done, and I will vouch for you that you will take good care of the baby."

Marge asked the all-important question: "Is the baby healthy?" Karen, who was apprehensive, said, "I have some bad news for you. The baby has some problems. It has a clubfoot due to the fact that the mother didn't use any prenatal care. Also I need to tell you that he could die due to some other problems, and that the doctors aren't having too much hope."

Marge felt like a rug had been pulled from underneath her, and she said, "Karen, I don't know what to do. I don't know if I can handle a baby like that. I don't even know when the good Lord above would take him away from me."

Karen, who hushed for a minute as if she was trying to think of something, said, "Well, if I were you, I wouldn't look a gift horse in the mouth and just go for it."

Marge smiled for a second and said, "You know what, you're right. I will talk to Cecile tonight when he gets home from work."

As Marge got off the phone with Karen, a big smile grew on her face. With the prospect of Cecile coming home from work, she decided that she would finish the laundry that she was doing, and that she had to fix him up a good meal to prepare him for the good news.

She hurried up and finished up the laundry, and as she sat down at the kitchen table, she thought about what she could fix for dinner. She muttered to herself, "Now what is Cecile's favorite?" And as she said this, a wonderful thought came to her. She knew that he liked steak and potatoes for dinner, and she thought a nice salad would put the finishing touches on what would be a wonderful dinner.

As the day progressed, and as she was putting the finishing touches on the dinner, a car pulled up in the driveway, and it was Cecile pulling into the drive. As Marge heard this, she moved at a faster pace to get the table ready. Cecile went through the kitchen door and said, "Well, beautiful, how are you this fine evening?" Marge, unusually sweet, said, "Now you just sit down here, and have a nice dinner. I know how tired you are, so I had a nice dinner already prepared for you."

Cecile looked at Marge strangely. "Marge, why are you acting so strangely today? Did you wreck the car or whatever? What is going on in that sweet little head of yours?"

Marge looked at him lovingly and said, "Well now Cecile; I'm not up to anything, but I do have some good news for you."

As she said this, Cecile looked at her strangely, and said, "Well, what is it so I can say no real fast."

Marge looked at him and laughed. "I don't think that you'll say no to this Cecile." "I don't know about that now, but you can try me."

As Marge was putting his food on the plate, she said, "Well, do you remember Karen?" "Why, yes, I know her. So, what of it?"

Marge looked at him as if to say, *Boy are you dense*, but she continued on. "Well, you know that we can't have any children. And you promised me that we could adopt a child."

Cecile, staring at her, said, "I know what I promised you."

Marge just knew that she was going to have a hard time with this one, as she went on. "Karen told me that there was a baby born a week ago, and it's just laying there in a crib, just waiting to be plucked like a fruit from a tree."

Cecile was finding it hard to catch up. Finally something came through, and he said, "You mean that I have a chance to become a father?"

"That's right, Cecile, we have a chance to adopt a precious life, and it's just waiting."

Cecile said, "Now I have another question for you, is the baby healthy?"

Marge felt a little nervous because, she didn't know how he would feel about the baby's condition, but she knew that she had to tell him the truth. "Well, I have some bad news in that regard; the baby came out with his feet backwards, according to Karen. The mother was an alcoholic and she didn't use any kind of prenatal care, and that's one of the problems."

Cecile said, "Go ahead and tell me more, because this don't sound so good."

Marge said, "Well, there is more. It seems that the baby isn't eating any food either. It seems that it has been days since the baby ate anything."

Cecile suddenly put down his fork on his plate and said, "Now I know why I'm getting all of this attention. You want to adopt this baby with a lot of health problems, don't you?"

Marge said, "Cecile, I don't ask for much, and you know that I take care of you well, and that I clean the house and everything, and I wouldn't mind at all taking care of this little one. And besides, I think there is a chance that it will be all right, and I'm willing to take a chance."

Cecile said, "Sometimes in life honey, you have to take chances in life, and that's why I'm going to support you in any way possible. I want to be a good husband to you, and I know that I promised this baby to you, and I just want you to know that if something should happen to this baby, I'll be there for you."

As Marge leaped up into the air, she said, "I just know that you won't be sorry, for I intend to raise this baby right, and I am also here to tell you that I love you forever for doing this fine thing for me."

,"I am going to love being a father to this little one, and sometimes in life, beggars can't be choosers, and who knows, he may grow up to be the captain of the football team." As Cecile said this, both of them fell into each other's arms and hugged.

Marge said, "I will call Karen right now, and find out when we need to go to the hospital, and do whatever we have to do."

As she went to the phone to call Karen's office, she picked up the receiver and as she dialed the number, the phone clicked and as the other end rang another voice soon came on the other end, and said, "This is Karen Baker Hospital, can I help you?" Marge excitedly said, "Karen, this is Marge; and I just got through talking over it with Cecile, and I have some good news for you, Cecile has just agreed with me, and that we want to adopt that precious little one that you have over there." Karen didn't respond right away, and then said, "I'm glad for you, and that I think that you should come right over here in the morning and come in and claim this little one." Marge said, "We will be there when you come in, so that you can help us." Karen said, "that will be fine, and so then; I hope to see you first thing in the morning, and Marge you won't be sorry; again thank you."

After Marge got off the phone, she told Cecile, "I have everything set up and we're ready to roll."

"I'm a father!"

Marge looked at Cecile with a look of concern, as he had a pale look on his face. "Cecile, you look as though you might need a doctor."

"It's just that it's a new thing for me," Cecile said.

"I know that it is, but look at the advantages of being a father," Marge replied. Cecile stared into space and smiled at the prospect of it.

Both of them didn't get a wink of sleep that night. The next morning, they knew that it would be a long day for them. The weather outside was not cooperating at all, for it was cold and a light rain was falling.

As they pulled into the drive, Karen came out to greet them. "Hey you two, I'm glad to see you here today."

"Karen, it's colder than a well digger's shovel out here. Can we forget the formalities and get on with paper work?" Marge asked.

Karen laughed and said, "Of course, you need to come inside where it's warm as well." Cecile said, "I can go for that." And as they laughed, because, they all knew what a special moment it would be when all of the paper work would be done, and when the baby got well, as they would be able to bring the baby home. As they entered the double doors, and made a turn to the left where the administration offices were, a young black lady, who was very nice to them said, "I'm Mrs. Wentworth, and I just want to congratulate you on the first steps of being parents." Marge said, "We are so excited because we didn't get a wink of sleep last night, didn't we dear?" Cecile, who also looked the worse for the wear said, "I am exhausted but yet I feel good all over." And as they laughed, they continued into the office where Mrs. Wentworth proceeded to gather the necessary paper work to handle the case. She said, "Now you know that there is a six-month waiting period before this adoption can come through, right?" Marge and Cecile looked at each other, and said, "We want to do what is necessary to get this precious life." Mrs. Wentworth looked pleased as they said it at the same time; that meant the couple was on the same page. After a while of filling out the paper work, Marge asked, "May we see the baby?" Mrs. Wentworth said, "I don't see any problem why you shouldn't." And as she said this, she ordered Karen to show them where the baby was. They walked at a fast pace, both dying to see the little one, and slowly approached the crib. Karen picked up the baby and said, "Here is the little one, and I'm getting jealous, because I have been in charge of taking care of this little one, and here you are taking him away from me." Marge said, "Well, Karen, when I knew that this little one was available, I just knew that I wanted it." Karen said, "How does it feel holding this little one? Here Cecile, hold your future son." And as Marge handed the baby gently to Cecile, he noticed that the baby smiled at him, and he said, "Marge, my son smiled at me as if he knew that I am going to be his father." Marge said, "Oh Cecile, don't you know that babies develop gas in their system, and they just do it.' "No, Marge!" As he stood there holding the precious little life before him, he said, "I am telling you that he smiled at me." Marge said, "Oh, come on, Cecile, let's get out of here so that Karen can go back to work." And as she grabbed him by the arm, the baby was put back into the crib, and they took off, saying goodbye to Karen.

A few months have passed and the adoption went through with no problem. And pretty soon, I was finally able to go to my new home; but if you want to know anything more about how they were or not able to straighten out my foot problem, you just have to read the sequel to this one to find out.

The neighborhood kids and I formed a club. The club was based on our favorite TV show, *Dark Shadows*, and it used to come on CBS every day at 4 p.m. We would meet at 4:30 to discuss what happened that day and what would happen on the next episode tomorrow. We would meet to see who would be right and why. It was a time for us to be together. Afterwards, we would have to go do our homework, and our parents made sure it got done. During the meeting, the club would ask me if I was going to play football in the upcoming season. I would tell them that I didn't know because my parents would kill me. The club then would ask me, "Well, you mean your dad wouldn't be proud of you out there on the football field?" I said, "I think my dad would be all right with it, but I don't think my mom would be too keen on the idea." But as friends go, they encouraged me to do it because they know that I'm that good of a player. So I decided that I would talk to Dad, and maybe he would be able to talk to Mom about what would be the best thing for me and how it would be the right thing to do.

After I got home and while we were setting the dinner table, I decided to bring up the subject. "I wanted to ask you all something. I decided that I want to play football, and I wanted to know if it would be all right for me to go ahead and try out for the team."

Then there was the time in my young life that I experienced something strange. When the day approached, we were watching the news on the TV because they would do coverage of the solar eclipse.

We would be standing outside waiting on that particular spot where it would be easy to see. Sure enough, it would be scary to see a black circle coming in an average type of speed. When it would come close to the sun, it would come to a screeching halt, and then it would slowly start to cover the sun. Soon, it would be dark outside as if it was nighttime.

One day my mom called for me while I was watching the parade fly over the house. I answered, "Coming, Mom!" I walked into the house, and as I entered the kitchen, she was sitting at the kitchen table. She said, "Come here, son, and let me tell you something." As I sat, she said, "I don't know how you feel, but you know that you are old enough to make your own decisions. This one is very important and could change your life." As I listened to her, I realized that it was about my foot, so I told her, "Mom, I have a feeling that this is about my deformity. I want to tell you that it is all right and that I'm willing to do whatever it takes to get my life back to normal." My mother smiled and told me, "So, is it all right that I call the doctor back and make the appointment?" I looked at her and said, "Sure, I'm ready to go as long as it means no school." My mom looked at me and said, "You!"

The appointment was made, and the day of the operation fast approached. When I slowly woke up from the Novocain, I was lying in the hospital bed with a cast on my leg, and there was my mom right by my side. I realized that Dad was working to pay the bills, but I knew he would be along later after he got off.

The only thing that I remember about the cuisine of the hospital was my saying, "Yuck," and there was an affirmative from my mom. But she encouraged me to eat the meals because if I didn't they wouldn't ever let me out of there. After that pep talk, I began to devour the food before me. I wasn't thrilled about it, but if it would get me out of there sooner, then so be it.

After a period of six weeks of me being a good boy, I was finally going home, a word that I thought I would never hear again. When the car pulled into the drive, I was in a big hurry to get into the house. For a period of time, I would have to be in a wheelchair to get around.

It wasn't long before another summer vacation would start. It was time for the beaches and water parks to open once more. We were watching the news at the time, so we were aware that a hurricane was brewing off the coast and would be heading our way. Her name was Gracie, and it was soon going to impact our lives. It was a hectic time preparing for the storm. Knowing that we weren't going to evacuate, we did all the things that the news was telling us to do like getting water, canned goods, and other items that we needed to survive the storm. I would have nightmares about the storm, thinking it would be Godzilla coming ashore with his fiery breath and stomping Charleston into the ground. My parents would try to calm me down and tell me that there was nothing to worry about.

As the days approached, the weather started to get scary. I noticed that all the animals that lived in the back of the house were either gone or in hiding. It was so eerie to see the ominous clouds that started to gather even though the storm was still hundreds of miles off the coast. When the storm finally came ashore, the wind speed was clocked at eighty miles per hour, and pretty soon, all the power would be out in the area. During the night of the storm, you could not get any sleep because of the wind and the tornadoes that were tearing things up outside. It was a sleepless and scary night. Everyone tried to go to bed as the storm raged on, but then all of a sudden, it became quiet like it was over. It was eerie as we looked up and saw the stars in the sky, but it would only last for a few minutes before we started hearing rumbling far off. We figured we better head on inside for safety. The back side of the storm was heading our way, and I thought, "Here we go again." It sounded like there was a war going on. The radio was only picking up remote stations and since there was so much static, we decided to go back to bed and wait it out till the morning.

Finally, morning game, and it was such a beautiful sight to see the sun shine down and feel the heat of the sun once more. For a week, we camped out. I can remember the old little Coleman stove that we used to help us survive the ordeal. It was something to see my mom encourage me to take a sponge bath. I didn't like it one bit for the water was cold. I guess it would have to take a spanking in order for me to do it, or the threat of one. But after it was all said and done, it was an adventure. Due to the fact, I can now claim that I'm one to be scared of a hurricane. I'm amazed now that technology has advanced so much that you are so much safer in the storm.

After that week, things started to get slowly back to normal. It only took two weeks to restore power to our humble home. As far as the cleanup phase, it was also slow, but pretty soon it all would be back to normal. It would be nice to see the birds and all the animals come back again. I would be able to go outside again with no problem and all my favorite TV shows would be on again. It seems strange the things that you take for granted, but we all seem to. When things finally get back to normal and the lights come back on, you wind up saying, "Thank God!"

The most exciting time that I can remember was the time that we planned to go to see my aunt and uncle who lived in New York City. I can remember watching the story of Superman, who resided in the great city of Metropolis, and to me it was the same thing as New York City. It would be the most exciting vacation of all, seeing my parents packing clothes and deciding what to wear.

When the day finally came, it was a time of getting up early and traveling on the road. It would be quite an adventure, going from place to place, seeing all the strange sights and sounds. It would be especially beautiful to go up into the mountains and see the majestic view. And when you experience traveling along the east coast and witness its beauty, you can appreciate the song "America the Beautiful." Don't get me wrong. We're proud of our home state of South Carolina, but when you visit some of the sights and sounds of other places, you appreciate where you live even more as well as the privilege that you have and take for granted sometimes. But overall, I love America and always will.

When you finally drive into New York, you see all the tall buildings or skyscrapers that are prevalent all over. I can remember my eyes being wide open as I tried to absorb all the sights and sounds that were there. I also remember the first time that I rode the subway. To me it was an exciting time, but it was strange to see the people act so rudely to each other as they climbed aboard. There would be a guy there especially hired to make sure that you go in the back of the subway. He is known as the pusher. I know one thing for sure—he must enjoy making the people miserable, because he was so good at making people do what he said like he was in complete control. Maybe one of these old days in the future, I will have to go back, because there is no place on earth that is as exciting as New York.

As I tell you about my many adventures, I would have to take time out and tell you of a time when I was a young lad growing up. I liked to go out on a Saturday night to do a little drinking at the old watering hole. But after the incidents I told you about, I have turned away from all the foolishness. I have stayed on the right path of the Lord. I stay home on weekends at nights, but that is not to say that I live a life of a hermit. After all, I love the beach and going surfing. As you recall, I do a lot of physical activity, which helps to make me feel young. In fact, I like to say that even at my age now, I only feel 20 and am still kicking very strong. I loved the summer in the past, because at America's edge, which is considered Folly Beach, I would love to go to hear the beach bands. I would also take the time to take my surfboard out and go surfing with other locals. And we would play my all-time favorite sport, volleyball. We would have tournaments, and it would get very physical indeed, especially in front of the net when you play defense. I also like bowling and canoeing. We have such beautiful rivers here. I would love to go watch the snakes as they swim in the fiver and to aggravate the alligators. I would canoe close to them and poke them in the belly with my paddle to wake them up. They did not like it, so they would splash water and do their roll as if they were aggravated with me. Then I would row away from the big ape.

Soon fun would come to an end, and I would have to go back to work again. As I would always say: "Man, that Navy career sure does look nice now." I was old enough to do this, and with all my being I wanted to join the service. I had already talked to a recruiter. I was coming close to making a decision. But the recruiter was always agitating me on the phone, constantly reminding me I had a deadline to meet and needed to make up my mind.

The football team started preparing in August to play football in the fall. There would be a war of words between my mother and father about whether they would allow me to play. They had to sign a release form, which would allow me to play, but it would all hinge on whether or not my mom would break down and let me play.

All of the neighborhood kids knew what would be happening, so they would encourage me to fight for my right to play. Mom would just have to realize that football like any other sport is a type of game in which you or anyone could sustain any type of injury at any given moment. That is why we tried to emphasize to her that this is why we have coaches. Their job is to train us to be hard so that we can make it through the season. If we were to be hit in any given area, all we had to do is brush ourselves off and continue to play. But as you know, it's like telling your mom that when you're drafted into the armed forces, you would be coming home safely.

My favorite subjects in school were science and math. My teacher thought that I would be in the military or in some field like that because I was so strong in these subjects. I enjoy learning about history and appreciate the skills of our scientists who could invent such a thing as a spaceship that would eventually go to the moon. I could remember watching Walter Cronkite, who is retired now. I remember him on the TV, describing the events as they would unfold. I was fascinated and in awe of the risks that our guys would be taking. We were at odds at the time with a country named Russia. This was not a war of violence, let's say, but a race to see which one could land on the moon first. Walter Cronkite would have a model of the spaceship and would show what would be going on in each situation that would pop up if need be. I watched a lot of space missions, but the main one was coming up soon and that was the one to wait for. The moon mission was coming soon. I knew where I would be and that was in front of the TV.

The day finally came—the day of the moon mission. There would be drama in this one. It was always exciting to see the launch as it roars with a thunderous noise as it rises up in the air. It only took seconds for the ship to be in space.

It went on day after day, as the news media would describe the efforts of these men who would make history. From the launch to the landing on the moon, it was amazing how people would have the gift of building these machines of marvel that can withstand the elements of space and the radiation to explore strange new worlds, to seek out new life forms, to go where no man has gone before. Someone once said this on the TV (I guess you know who I mean), but isn't it amazing how they come up with these shows on the sci-fi scene and then later on in time, it can become reality?

I can still remember the old black-and-white TV, which showed the landing on the moon. As the spaceship would come down and as the dust settled, the term *touchdown* was blurted out. Then it was time to celebrate as the people who had worked so hard to put it together would be shaking hands and congratulating each other.

Later on in my adult life, I found out that the good doctor was running for political office. After all this time, I thought I had forgotten the pain of my granny's death, but all was for naught. I wish at times that I could forget the things he has done to the family, but alas, I shall not be able to forgive or forget.

And during the evening hours when I would watch the evening news and see him giving speeches that would try to convince people to vote for him, I knew in my heart that I would not vote for him. To this day, I sometimes think about why he would treat my granny in that way.

It seems as though I am not able to forget the bad times such as death. It seems that I won't ever be able to forget the death of any of my family. In my heart, I know that I'm repeating myself, but that is the anger that is stirring within me. I would always step back and try to forget, but the pain would always be there and I would always dream of different ways to torture him. But one of these days, I want to confront him one-on-one, and I would ask him why?

One day, as I looked through the paper, I noticed that he would be giving a speech on different issues, so I decided that I would join the little speech that he would be giving to the folks about why they should vote for him.

As I entered the auditorium, I noticed him, but he acted like he didn't even know me so I thought to myself that it would be to my advantage if he didn't know me. As the night progressed and the time to hear his boring speech approached, I calmly waited for the part where he would be accepting questions from the audience. This would be the time that I would stand up and tell him off about what I thought about him. It seemed as though as it got closer to the time to question, I was getting more and more excited about the prospect of telling him off. When it became time for him to start accepting questions from the audience, I still waited for the proper moment for me to ask the questions that I hoped would have changed the voters' minds about him. As he finished answering someone's question, I rose up and asked him, "Do you remember me?" As he looked at me, I could imagine just what the answer would be. And then he said, "No, son, I don't remember who you are."

I stood up and told him, "Well I guess that you have become such an important man about town that you have forgotten my granny who laid in bed suffering all night waiting for you to come to her aid, but I haven't." He looked hard in my face as if he could kill me and said, "Well if there are no more questions, I guess I could call it an evening." Someone called out, "Wait a minute here, aren't you going to ask the gentleman there a question or give him an answer to his question?" The future politician looked perplexed and looked as though he thought the situation was getting out of hand. He acted like he thought he could dodge the situation and said, "Now, who are you supposed to be?"

As he squinted in the back row, a person who was standing up looked right back at him and said, "I am a reporter who wants you to answer the young man's question." He tried to get a better look at him but he couldn't, so he said, "Well, you may not have listened, but I thought I gave the young man a sufficient answer for now." The reporter then asked, "Well, the last time I had my physical exam from my doctor, he told me that my hearing is fine and so I have to ask you—do you know that man who asked you that question?" The retired doctor didn't know what to say after that, so he said, "As I said, I answered the young man's question to the best of my ability and that I don't have to tell you a damn thing."

The reporter was not convinced, so he said, "I think that you're hiding something. I think that with a little probing around, I can find out what it is. And another thing, sir, I think that my readers would be very interested in knowing what this young man thinks about you."

When I woke up the next day, I scanned the paper to find out that I had made the front page of the local paper. I noticed that the headline read that the retired doctor had something to hide from his past. I had a smile on my face because I knew now that the pressure would be on him to show us the truth about himself. And I knew that my granny would be looking down on me right now, and she would be thanking me for a job well done on my part. All of a sudden, I jumped because the phone rang. The voice on the other end of the line said, "Hey? Do you remember me?" I thought about it a minute and then said, "Oh, I want to thank you for backing me up against him last night."

The voice on the other end of the line was the reporter who had backed me up and wanted to know what I knew of the good doctor. The reporter told me, "Well, I want to give you an interview so that you can tell all my readers what you know about the good doctor." I thought about it a short minute and told him, "I would be glad to tell you anything I could about it, and maybe the readers of your paper would think twice about voting for him for anything."

It was a rainy evening when I walked into the office of the good reporter, and as I walked into the office, a nice receptionist asked me who I was and so I told her. Naturally, the good reporter didn't leave her any word of my coming to see him. As we talked, the reporter stuck his head out of his office and said, "Hey, how about coming on in and let us talk some more about last night." As I entered his office, he was coming around the desk to sit down. As he looked at me, he said, "Now, what's your story?" I looked at him and said, "I and my family are a witness to the doctor's actions in the past, and let me tell you this, I wouldn't vote for him for dog catcher." The reporter smiled at me and said, "Well you tell me all about it, and I will tell all the people about the good doctor, and maybe we would be able to stop him from being the dog catcher." And as he said this, we both laughed.

In everyone's life, there is something that everyone must face, and that is death.

After calling the doctor and waiting for hours for him to give the final notice that she has passed on, the anger began as I wondered why she had to suffer like that. Why couldn't the doctor have come any sooner to ease her out of her misery? As we waited on the doctor, we felt that we could have lynched him for what he did to her.

Finally, he came through the door with the look on his face, which said "Why am I here?" And as he came through the door, he asked, "Where is the patient?" Well, when he asked such a stupid question, it made me want to kill someone with an attitude like that. My mom escorted him to the room where my grandmother was lying. After he had examined her on the bed and then laid the sheet on her, he got up and walked back to the room where we were sitting. He told us that she passed away and that he was sorry that it happened to such a good woman.

We looked at him like he was a dirt bag for telling us something that we already knew. But after he left and as they took the body away, all we could do at the time was hold each other and cry. I was pretty glad to see my dad come home, but at the same time, I would be pretty glad to see our other good home that I do call home. I somehow knew that there would be difficult days ahead, but somehow I also knew that we would prevail and we would overcome it. But I knew that there would always be hate in my heart for this man because deep in my heart I knew that he could have come sooner and eased some of her pain.

The pain that I was feeling at that time would be almost impossible for me to describe to you. You could not comprehend everything that was going on at one time. You look around and notice that your mother is crying, and something inside of you tells you that something is wrong. At this age, you just don't understand that word. Death in my opinion is always emotionally hard to deal with at any time. And when you are little, it is especially hard. My poor grandmother had lain in the bedroom screaming in pain and wishing that the pain would go away or that she could just end it all. We felt bad that we could eat something and she couldn't. All that she was able to do was scream.

From the time everything began happening to my grandmother, my mom would try to call the doctor. She would frantically be calling the office to complain that no one was coming by to help her in her hour of need. The only thing that the receptionist would say was that the doctor was busy at the time and would not be able to return her call, but the doctor would be getting all the messages that she left. My mom would hang up the phone and give me one of those looks that told me that things didn't look very good.

I guess I remember it so well because my mom's expression told me that the receptionist's tone of voice was very rude, and the look on my mother's face told me that there would be no help coming. As the screaming went on from day to day, it seemed like that it would never end. Finally, by the third night of this ordeal, my mom would start calling the doctor's house to see if she could leave word with his wife or him. She would ask if he would give her something for the pain that she would greatly appreciate it.

When she called, all she would get would be more abuse from the wife. All she would say was, "My husband is very busy, and we don't want you to call here again" or "My husband is busy resting and he doesn't want to be disturbed at this time."

My mother was appalled when she heard this rude lady on the phone and said some rude words back to her when she hung up.

This is the story about the death of my grandmother who became very ill with liver cancer, which is a very painful way to pass on. It took me a very long time to get over my grandmother's death. Even to this day, I still think that I haven't gotten over it.

Let us go back in time to a period of my life in which I was eight years old. It was during the summer, and I was with my mother in the kitchen trying to fry up some scrambled eggs for us with which she would make a quick meal.

From my grandmother's bedroom, there came horrific screams of pain. They were screams that I would never forget because of the agony and the suffering she had to endure at this time. I became distressed over her anguish and felt helpless because there was nothing I could do to make her feel better.

It felt like I was waiting for the hurricane to strike at a city and as it would blow through the night, a look of horror would be showing on my face. My mother, who I remembered going through this with such bravery, would be getting her as comfortable as she could by using washcloths to ease her high fever, but she just kept screaming for her life. By the fifth day, the screaming stopped. My mom knew that my grandmother was gone. She gave me one of those looks and gave me a hug, because she knew what she would find when she walked back there. Then she approached the room and when she got closer to the bed, she started crying because when she felt my grandma, she knew in an instant she was gone. So she closed her eyes and gave her a kiss on the hand before she became even more emotional. As I heard her crying, I was too scared to walk to join her because I was too afraid of what I may find. But after a while, she finally walked out of the room and told me, "Son, I have some terrible news I have to tell you. Your grandma has gone to heaven." As she said those words, I darted out of the house somewhere to cry and to think of nothing but her. It would be a hard time in my life, because she had such a special place in my heart.

Every day as my grandmother's condition got worse; my dad would call my mom and check on her to see if she was all right. Dad could tell that my mom would be tired, and sometimes when he could, he would see after her and my grandmother. He couldn't do this all the time because he was part of the security force of the old Navy base, and it was sometimes a grueling job where he would work sixteen-hour shifts. He knew in his heart that his mom would be passing on very soon. He could not understand sometimes which was worse—the fact that his mother was dying or the knowledge of how hard it would be afterward when she would be gone. All he knew was that he would have to be there to support both of us and give us all the love that he could muster.

When someone dies in the family, it seems to bring out the worst in people. They just want to take everything someone owns. For instance, I know for a fact, that my granny wanted everything to go to my uncle, but for some unknown reason, there would be a battle for the possession of her property. Since there was no will to explain her wishes, there would be a fight among the family of who gets what. In the time of us needing the family to be together, it seems as though the family would be ever more apart.

I felt for my dad because he was the one who took such good care of my granny. And when he worked long hours at the office, Mom and I would be taking care of granny all during the day and night. Not one of the other family members had even been there to help with anything. We even bought the groceries for ourselves and for her so that she could eat something. There was no thought of anything that we did for her. Everything was to be all for them. It seems like times like these will bring out the worst in people and not the better, meaning that at times such as these, it should bring a family closer together. But more times than I can count or understand, it never works out that way. I am always amazed of the backstabbing that goes on in situations such as this. The only thing that I did know is that, I would always hate the man that would not even come to my grandmother's house to comfort her or ease her pain. And I know I always would have contempt for him. I just hoped that sometime down the road one of his family members would have something wrong with them and that they would not be able to go get anyone to help him.

There is a time in everyone's life where thoughts turn to love. When I was a freshman in high school, I already had thoughts of marriage. My mom would giggle at me and say, "You are way too young to think about such things." Why is it that parents always say that you are too young? I wonder, when they were my age, did their parents say the same thing? Anyway, I was falling for a beauty named Amber, who was talented and smart. Amber was always kind and had a good heart, but she didn't seem to like me. Another girl liked me, and I seemed to be in my own soap here. The other girl had a selfish streak in her. She was the type that our class just didn't like, but it was so hard to tell her that the answer was no! I found out that Amber felt the same way about me because one morning before class started, the two girls fought over me. I found out by asking what was going on as the two fought, and one of the students looked at me and said that they were fighting over me. I was shocked to say the least, but I knew that my decision would be very simple.

The next day after the fight, I finally decided that I was going to have a talk with Amber to see what the ruckus was about. As Mom dropped me off at the school, I ran toward her and said, "Hey, what are you up to, pretty lady?" Amber looked at me and smiled as she started to walk away. I said, "Wait a minute. What did I do? I want to see if I can help." She stopped, turned around, and finally said, "What is this? I hear that you and Gloria are going together?" I was shocked to say the least about her statement and said, "I'm not interested in Gloria. I'm only interested in you at this time, and I want to take you out after school." Amber, who now was shocked, said, "You want to see me? I was always under the impression that since Gloria was always chasing you around that you would be a couple." I laughed out loud after she said that and said, "You have got to be kidding! I have always had a crush on you, but I was too shy to ask you out till now. I didn't know how you felt about me until yesterday!" Amber started laughing, and we both started walking together and had a conversation about what our plans were going to be for that weekend. But at a distance, a very angry Gloria was standing and listening. She now knew the truth, and she vowed that she was going to get even with me. As far as Gloria, I guess she decided to leave things alone and give us a chance to go our separate ways. We were *the* couple that year, and as far as I was concerned, it would always be that way. I think Amber felt the same way, but today we don't keep up.

However, there was another time and another place for another love to come our way as in each school year that comes along. People get tired of one another and move on. This is how I asked my girlfriend to marry me. During the afternoon when I got off at the base, I decided to go to the jewelry store and buy her the most expensive engagement ring that money could buy. I thought she would be worth the expense. When I entered the store, a very nice lady was at the counter to help me. I asked her, "Yes ma'am, I'm interested in one of those engagement rings, and I think that this one on the corner that is so bright is the one that I want." She told me, "Why yes, sir, that is a beautiful ring, and it will complement her beauty." I said, "I agree completely with you on her being beautiful, and yes, I also agree with you that that this ring would be perfect for her." She then asked, "Sir, what size did you want?" I told her, "I think that she would be a size seven and would you mind wrapping it for me?" She smiled and proceeded to do as I instructed her. When she handed it to me and as I paid for it, I had confidence that everything would work out."

Later on that evening, I stopped off at her place and knocked on her door. She opened the door and said, "Well, come on in, handsome." As I entered I asked her, "Well, Beautiful, are you ready to go?" She told me, "I will be as soon as you help me zip this dress up." I took the zipper with my fingers, raised it up, and fastened it. Then I said, "Well there you are, ma'am." She turned around and said, "Well, how do I look?" I told her, "You look simply ravishing, my dear." She giggled and took me by the arm as if she was ready to go, but I hesitated and told her, "Hey, can we sit down a minute?" She shook her head yes and said, "What's the matter? Are you all right?" I told her, "There is something I wanted to ask you, and now seems to be a good time." I reached into my pocket and said, "Miss Sarah Martinez, will you do me the honor and marry me?"

As Sarah and I prepared to leave the great state of Florida, Sarah became depressed about leaving her home. At first, it was the idea of leaving something that you are used to being in a strange place and with strange people. I tried to convince her that my hometown of Charleston, South Carolina was a nice, friendly place to live. The weather during the summer time can get pretty sticky, but mostly, you will be around people who will love you and around family.

She then sighed as if to tell me that she didn't believe me, but I told her, "Now listen to me honey, it will be all right. You are going to love our home that will be waiting; and also when you start to learn your way around the area, you are going to love swimming in the beaches and water parks. And when other places are having snow all winter, you can brag and tell your folks that you're basking in the sun and enjoying a seventy-degree climate. Let them know that you're very happy here, and when they hear how great our city is, maybe they would like to come down and stay with us."

She felt better and better, and by the time the plane landed in the Charleston Airport, she wore a big smile on her face. She was more like her old self.

After a period of time, things were back to normal, and Sarah was beginning to enjoy the edge of America so much that she would almost be living at the beach, basking in the warm sun as I went to work. As she went to do her shopping, she noticed that the people were friendly, and that when we went to dine in the restaurants around the area, she would notice that they provided good service and that they were very friendly. And there was more news. We would be at odds when college football started because she was a fan of the Florida State Seminoles and naturally I was a fan of the South Carolinas Gamecocks.

It would be a proud day for my dad, who was in town for the graduation ceremony. He bragged to everyone there that he would be in town for the naval ceremony to honor those who passed their induction to the Navy. I couldn't believe it myself. I survived everything that they could dish out, and there I was, a crippled boy who had a clubfoot, wearing a uniform of the United States Navy. Who would have thought that I would come to this point? I was thinking about everyone in high school and of all my teachers who taught me who did not think that I would be able to make it this far. Not only that, I had heard from Mom, who acted like she was in shock that I would make the military. Yes, I would be proud to march in the parade today. I was so glad that, by tonight, all of us with our parents had the freedom to tour the city that we haven't had a chance to explore. It seemed like you were in prison for the duration, and you aren't able to escape until you are paroled. And today is the day to let your hair hang down and party hearty, as they say.

As we lined up outside in our sharp new uniforms, we could now say that we were Navy men, ready to do any assignment that our commander had before us. He had all the confidence in the world in us—the young men and women who would go forth and serve this great country of ours. And as he told the audience, "Here is your next line of defense. Here are your next graduates of the United States Navy." And as he said that, everyone took out their white caps and threw them in the air. It was finally over.

As the ceremony grew to a close, my mom and dad finally found where I was, and my mom could not recognize me. She said, "Cecile, who is this fine young man standing before me? I'm not sure, but is this my son?" My dad laughed and said, "Why Marge, do you mean to tell me that you don't recognize your own son?" Marge, looking at me in my sharp polished uniform, said, "No, I don't. This can't be my son. He looks so polished and strong." And as the Navy man and gentleman that I was, I said, "This is what the military does to you, Mom. It makes a man out of you, and now I have some more news. Dad, I have been assigned to be in intelligence. I promised you I would follow in your footsteps and now I am." Dad couldn't believe it. He had tears running down his cheeks and shook my hand and patted me on the back at the same time. As we left the base, I could not help but look back and remember all the hell I had to go through. I began to think how it was well worth it, and I had a big smile on my face when the CO was shaking a few hands. He returned the smile back.

One night as I stood quartermaster watch, I noticed that one of the people who were waiting to be kicked out of the Navy had signed the sheet in order to use the bathroom and was taking an extremely long time in the bathroom. In these quarters, the windows had not only iron bars but also a mesh to prevent escape. As I entered the bathroom, I noticed that somehow the mesh was cut and the iron bars had somehow been pried apart. I immediately started to blow my whistle and run outside to warn the sentry that we had someone trying to escape. And as he ran to the wall, the sentry had a weapon on him. When he noticed the young man trying to escape, he opened fire on the young man and shot him in the butt, which was a good thing because he was getting ready to climb over the wall. That would be as much excitement as I could stand for one night. And I would gladly to report to my bunk and try to get at least a couple of hours of sleep.

The next morning came, and I was up at the usual time. And as usual, they inspected us as far as person, bunk, and clothes, and then after we were noted as passed, my CO walked up to me and told me, "I wish you good luck today, because I noticed that you have been studying so I know that you will pass your two final exams." I nodded my head in agreement and said, "I hope that I can do well for you, sir!" He smiled and patted me on the back.

I entered the building in which I was going to take my test, and I won't lie to you. I was very nervous. But when the instructor passed out the reading test, I had a big smile on my face for I knew that it would be a piece of cake.

After you read a passage from the test, it would have on the bottom of the page a selection of answers. The way I figured it, if they were going to time me and give me only thirty minutes to complete this thing, I would not read the entire passage. I would just read the question first and then I would go ahead and hunt for the answer in the passage. As I read each question, I knew with every strike of my pencil that I had the right answer, and I knew I would pass that part of the task at hand to be in the Navy, which was my destiny.

As we were getting back to base, they were weighing all the other teams. As it turned out, a lot of them had lost several pounds, but when it came to us, the CO noticed that our weight was the same. The CO had questions for us, but when I explained how we survived, he was quite pleased and congratulated us on passing our survival. The next item on our list would be the swimming test. I hated that because I was kind of nervous about being in the water. The lady instructor, later on that week, would say, "Now gentlemen, I don't see any ladies on board, or do I? Well, we have to wait and see if you earn the title of being a lady, after this. What I want you to do is to dive off that diving board, and when you do so, you must tread water until we say stop, and when you finish this, you must swim all the way to the other side of the pool. Do you understand?" Everybody yelled as if they did. There were a few of the guys who could not make it because you had to tread water for a very long time. But, the rest of us made it quite well. And we all were glad that it would be over with, except for the fact that the Navy could give you three strikes or you would not make the challenge of being a Navy man. And we felt for those who had to do it all over again. Then all of a sudden, the lady instructor came out and said, "Now you must learn the fine art of going underwater and taking the clothes off your back and using them as life preservers. As you know, water fills your pants and your denim shirt, and it makes a floatable life-saving device. This comes in handy whenever you might be thrown overboard or your ship has an accident or when you are in combat, God forbid, and it might sink in the middle of nowhere." She further said, "I hope that this will never happen, but we want you to be prepared in case of any emergency that might occur." We were ordered to go back into our dressing rooms and prepare for the second phase of our swim test.

When we came out of the dressing rooms, we would have our dry uniforms on but pretty soon, we had to get used to a different ball game as we were lining up to take another dip in the pool. This was a little scary because we were submerged underwater, even though the test was supervised by a diver who would make sure that we would not get in any trouble. And the diver would help us in case we got stuck because it would be important to take as little time as possible since you can only breathe for so long. As each of us was completing the second phase of this test, some of us realized that we were not water persons and therefore would have to take this test all over again. I, however, appreciated where I came from more and more. For you see that when you live in Charleston, South Carolina, you are surrounded by the ocean and beaches. I was glad that not only was I a certified diver but that I also loved to surf and dive as well. In fact, a lot of our area oceans are so beautiful to explore, especially with all the Civil War artifacts that would be down on

the bottom of the Ashley River. It was amazing to be
surrounded by so much history. Again, I am proud to be
a good Sandlapper.

As I drove in and went under the water, the diver was
with me. I was amazed at how fast I caught on to what
they instructed us to do. And as usual, I would come out a
winner, and I would pass the swim test. As I came up out
of the water, I told the diver, "A piece of cake my man,
and it was good to meet you!" The diver smiled back and
as the CO was briefed on how they thought I was doing,
he said, "I'm going to pay attention to this young man,
Mr. Brady, and I am going to make sure that he makes
it. I know that he has worked so hard for this, and he is
close to making it. He has met every goal the has come to
him, and he will study and work hard to pass the reading
test and the maritime history test, and I think that should
about do it except for the chamber test next week and
then graduation." Everyone agreed with his assessment
of the situation at hand. I would have a handful of tests in
the upcoming weeks, and I would have guard post duty.
They put me on the toughest guard duty assignment
of all. And that would be guarding the weirdos in the
nuthouse to try to keep them from escaping and going
over the wall. "Are we going to have fun in the old town
tonight?" I would say to myself. I wasn't looking forward
to guarding this place for I would be all alone with no
gun. What was amazing was they would know that and
try every trick in the book to escape. And no matter how
hard you wanted to sleep, you must not or that would be
trouble. I was not looking forward to this, and with all
the studying I had to do, I didn't know if I could keep up

the pace at this point of the ball game. The only think I knew was that I just couldn't let my dad down, because, after all, I wanted to follow in his footsteps.

I had to admit I was pleased with the move that we made back into the low country because I would be back in the woods during the summer hunting deer. And when springtime came around, I would also get back to hunting the elusive wild turkey. Believe me, not only are they challenging to hunt, but they are a challenge you can call close enough so that you can get a good aim at it and shoot. In addition, I was getting back into the summer thing when I could take the wife along on the boat and go fishing. She would enjoy crabbing more than fishing, but I stayed with the fishing. Like all relationships, everyone can't agree on everything, but I always wore a smile when my mom and she would get together. She finally admitted to me that it would be like I said it would and that she was glad to make the move with me. I was pleased as punch that the family was able to accept her and love her just like I did.

However, there would be an event in my life that I wouldn't quite accept. One night while returning home from work, I noticed that my wife was treating me nicely, so I was wondering if she had wrecked the car or bought something that was too expensive. It was a nice dinner and afterwards she said, "Oh dear, by the way…" When she said that I cringed, wondering what would be next. Then I found out when she said, "I told you awhile back that I had my physical today from the doctor. He told me some good news that I thought I should pass on to you." I hesitated for a couple of minutes and said, "What would that be dear?" She kind of smiled and said, "Now don't use that tone with me, Scott. What I wanted to tell you was that the doctor told me that I was pregnant." When she told me that, I hit the ceiling with joy. I hugged her and said, "You did it. I'm so thrilled. Just wait until Mom and Dad find out that they are going to be grandparents. Honey, you've made me the happiest man on the earth, and I promise that I'm going to help any way I can. There is one more thing I have to tell you." Looking concerned, she said, "And what is that dear?" I smiled and said, "I'm so proud that you are my wife, and that I would marry you twenty times over, and that I'm never sorry of the day that I said 'I do.' And that I love you very much." And when I grabbed her to give her a bear hug, she told me, "Hey, take it easy dear." I told her, "I can't take it easy. I have to do something to work off all this excitement built up in me." She told me, "Well, why don't you take Buster and go into the woods and go hunting? That always seems to cheer you up, especially when you bring back something." I told her, "You know what? You have something there. I think I will do just that!" Oh, I felt great, and I felt blessed that my wife would give me the greatest gift of all.

When we told our parents about what had happened, they were excited. My dad was very proud of the fact that I was doing so well in my life. So, when the next morning came, it would be an early start because all the trucks would be showing up to start building our new son's room. We really didn't expect them to show up so soon, but when they did, we rolled out of bed sleepy eyed. As the doorbell rang, I opened the door to find out that it was the builder. He said, "Mr. Brady, we are here to start on your extension." When he said this, I told him, "We're not dressed yet, but give us a few minutes and we would like to see it as they come up with it." He smiled, laughed, and said, "Why sure, you are quite welcome to observe the quality of our work." As they got started, we went outside because we were anxious to see the room completed; however, we knew that its completion would take a long time. Overall, it would be exciting to see the building come up. I hadn't told her yet, but I had already called a furniture store and bought the furniture for the baby's room. I didn't know how to sneak the furniture in yet, but I was kind of constructing a plan in my head. I figured that I had a while before the room would be completed, so I thought that I would have plenty of time.

Well, you heard the old saying. I think it went—-the best laid plans of mice and men. The builder told me, "With the good weather and everything, we are going to be through sooner than expected." With these words coming out of his mouth, I figured I needed to talk to my mom and dad quick.

I walked very fast into the living room while my wife was talking to the workers, giving them some insight or her opinions of the way she wanted things. I picked up the phone, called my mom and said, "Mom, I need your help to keep Sarah busy. Can you do that for me?" My mom said, "Why sure, son, there is plenty I could do to keep her busy with such as shopping and other stuff that we can do together." I told my mom, "I'm so glad that you said that because I need to put the furniture in the baby's room sooner than expected, and I need your help to keep her busy so that this will be a complete surprise to her." My mom agreed and told me, "Just let me know when they finish the room, and I can start keeping her busy while you do your thing. Oh! By the way, would you like Cecile's help?"

I told her, "I sure would appreciate it if Dad could because some of the stuff that I'm getting will be very heavy." Mom told me, "Well don't you worry, son. I think that I can talk to your father into doing that for you." I was hoping that the plan would work and work without a hitch.

Sure enough, the day came that the room was finished and the plan had to go into action. So, from my office, I called home and told Mom to start getting Sarah busy because it was time to start putting the furniture together. I wanted it to be arranged in a tasteful manner and I thought, knowing her as well as I did, that she would be pleased with how I fixed the room for the baby.

My mom started right away, and finally it was the day that the furniture would be delivered to the room. My Dad and I were ready to go and that I was so glad that my CO gave me the time off to plan this together with my dad. The phone rang and Sarah would pick up the phone and say, "Hello." My mom would reply, "Get yourself together, gal. We are going shopping." Sarah was taken by surprise and said, "Mom, now isn't the time. I have so many things to do, and I just don't know where to begin." My mom said, "I'm not going to take no for an answer. You have got to get some new clothes for yourself because you will be getting bigger soon." Sarah, who could never refuse my mom, told her, "You know, this can probably wait, and I thank you very much for doing this for me." My mom replied, "You are quite welcome, and besides, you are having my grandchild." Pop and I parked the car where we could see Mom pick up Sarah. We were ready to move into action.

Mom pulled into the drive, and we saw Sarah get into the car. We waited for them to pull out. It seemed to take forever, but finally they did. I looked at Dad and said, "Hey Dad, why do women take so long on doing anything?" My dad looked at me and said, "I don't know son. I guess that's women for you, but don't ever let me tell your mother that." I told him, "I sure won't tell Mom anything, Dad." We laughed together as we and the furniture truck that was following us started toward the driveway. As we pulled into the drive, the furniture truck took a left turn and pulled along side the house. The men came out of the truck, opened the back, and started to roll out the furniture. I was glad to see that the plan was going so well. I couldn't wait for Sarah to see the completed room when she got back with Mom.

When Mom and Sarah got back, Sarah noticed that Dad and I were there. Naturally, the furniture truck was already gone, and we were hurrying on the inside, trying to finish up. We had a huge curtain covering the door to the room, and we also had a red ribbon across the door. As Mom and Sarah came into the house, we had big smiles on our faces like we couldn't keep anything a secret. Sarah looking at Mom and at us at the door and said, "What in the world are you two up to?" I told her, "Well, dear, there is nothing going on that I can see. Right, Pop?" Pop said, "No son, I don't see anything going on around here." Sarah, looking at the huge curtain covering the door to the baby's room, said, "I'm talking about the huge curtain that is draped behind you." I turned around and said, "Oh! You mean this curtain. I don't know, but maybe this envelope might explain things." As she opened and read it, it told her to pull up the curtain and see what is behind it.

Sarah walked slowly towards the curtain, looked at both of us, smiled, and said, "I am scared to do this because I think you're up to something." I told her, "No, nothing evil is going on dear. Just pull the curtain as the note told you. I think that you are going to cry when you see this." As I said that, she finally reached out and pulled the curtain down, and saw the ribbon on the door.

My dad gave her a pair of scissors to cut the ribbon with. As she nervously cut the ribbon and opened the door, she gasped as she looked inside and saw the baby's room completed and filled with furniture. She looked at me and said, "Scott, it looks lovely. Thank you! How did you plan all this without me knowing about it?" I told her, "Well, it took a lot of planning, and with Mom's help, it went on without a hitch. She looked at Mom and said, "I'm going to see that I have to keep my eye on you from now on." Mom laughed and said, "It was my pleasure to do it for my favorite daughter-in-law and for my grandson." "It is so beautiful I could cry." Mom took Dad to the side and said, "Come on Cecile, let's go and leave them alone." Dad said, "I think you have seen enough. Now come on, old man, and let's go home." As they left, Sarah and I were kissing, and my mom looked at us and said, "I think before long, there will be two." I was just glad that everything went okay.

Since my wife was in her delicate condition, I decided to take the doctor's advice and told Sarah, "I think it would be a good idea for us to walk in the mall so that you will be healthy for the baby's sake and yours." Sarah agreed with me, and so the next morning, we started a habit of exercising. I wanted her to be ready, because the doctor told me that having a baby was painful and that walking each day would most likely keep the pain down when she gave birth.

While we were walking in the mall, I felt someone brush me, and I knew in an instant that someone was trying to steal my wallet. I immediately ran after him to subdue him, and I tackled him in front of all the shoppers. As I was putting the cuffs on him, I said, "I guess pal, that this is not your lucky day, now is it?" The guy just looked at me like he could kill me. I told everyone that I was a Navy intelligence officer and that I had the authority to arrest the man. As I walked through the crowd, everybody clapped and then my wife caught up.

I took my prisoner to the mall security office, so that they could call the police in order for me to process charges against him. As I entered the office, there was a sergeant at the desk, writing some information on a form. He looked up at me and at the prisoner and said, "Well, what do we have here?" I told him, "I'm a Navy CID officer, and I caught this pick pocket working the mall, and unfortunately, he picked me to try to steal my wallet." The desk sergeant said, "We have been getting complaints from the customers about missing purses and such. So this is him, huh? Well, I'll call the police and have them get him." I thought to myself I didn't have to write any reports on my day off. The desk sergeant grabbed the phone in front of him and began to make the call, and when the desk sergeant of the police answered, the mall security said, "Hey, I have a purse snatcher and a pick pocket that was messing with our customers here, but his luck ran out today. He tried to lift the wallet of a Navy CID officer, who apprehended him, and we're holding him for you as we speak." The police officer on the other end said, "Is he willing to press charges, and is he willing to testify against him?" The mall security officer said, "That is affirmative, officer. He would be willing to testify against him in court." The police officer said, "We will send a patrol car right away. Tell Mr. Brady thanks, and we will take it from here."

The mall security wanted my name and phone number to contact for trial, and I was glad to cooperate with them. As I walked out of the office, I spotted my wife in the food court area, eating an ice cream cone. I walked over to the table where she was sitting and said, "I always knew that you had a sweet tooth." She laughed and said, "I think that is the reason you married me, wasn't it?" I replied, "Sure, I knew you were sweet in there." I told her, "I will have to testify against him for trying to steal my wallet, and I think he would be put away for a long time."

I had my hunting clothes on and grabbed my rifle, and as I walked out of the door, I grabbed my wife and gave her a big bear hug. As I did so, she started laughing. I told her, "You know, I feel selfish now. Here you are pregnant, and I'm going hunting. I'm not sure that I should leave you alone right now." Sarah giggled and said, "Hey, I'm not at that stage yet, Scott. You go ahead and gave a good time. I'll be all right. Later on, down the road, I will need you." I couldn't help it, but I went ahead with my plan, and so I went into my truck and took off into the woods to work off the adrenaline that was inside me. The wife sat down on the couch in the living room and started to call Mom.

My mom answered the phone, "Hello, who's speaking please?" Sarah said, "Hey Mom, I'm so glad that I caught you. I have some news for you." There would be a hesitation on the line again, but finally, at the same time that Sarah took a deep breath to say something, my mom said, "You're not moving away again are you?" Sarah laughed and said, "Why mom, I am here to tell you right now that we are not moving, but—" Mom interrupted her. "Please tell me no buts, I can't handle any more moving by my son." Sarah laughs and said, "Now mom, if you would let me finish and let me tells you this great news, I'm going to bust like a little girl with a big secret." After saying this, my mom said, "What secret is this? What are you trying to tell me?" Mom," Sarah replied, "I'm going to give you a great gift. I'm going to have your grandchild.

There was a very nervous reply by my mom to the point that she could barely speak. But the words finally came out, "I'm so excited for you. When did you hear this?" Sarah, smiling, said, "I just learned about it this morning after I had my physical. The doctor wanted me and Scott to be together when they did an ultrasound on me to find out what it will be." After hearing the news, my mom was excited and told her, "I can't wait till your dad comes home to tell him that he's a grandfather."

Sarah said, "I wonder how he's going to react about being a granddad." My mom replies, "Oh, I'm pretty sure, he's going to be excited about it, and he would want to talk to Scott." My mom said, 'Where's Scott? Does he know yet? And how did he take the news." Sarah giggled and said, "You know what, he does know, but you know where he went?" My mom replied, "No, where did my son get to?" Sarah told her, "The first thing that son of yours did was grab his rifle and take to the woods." My mom took a deep breath, as if to say she didn't believe it. Sarah said, "Really he knows, and he was real excited about the prospect of being a father, and to be truthful he was so excited and wanted to stay with me, but I told him to go into the woods and relax, that I would be all right." My mom was relieved to hear that.

I was in my camo gear, waiting on and calling a particular bird. He would be a whopper of a turkey, at least twenty pounds. After being out there for a while, I started to hear him call back to me. I responded back, more frequently now, because the way I was taught by my father is that when you hear the bird call back, you respond immediately. You see, this would be the mating season for the bird, and you're ready and available to him. This routine always gets the poor thing in trouble, and I was hoping that I would nail the big bird today. I have been after him for a long time now, and today would be the day.

I was beginning to hear him call back to me more frequently now, and the main point of the story is that he was getting closer and closer to me with each call. Pretty soon, I should be able to see him in the clearing in front of me now. I also hoped that there would be no other wild animal around such as a bobcat or some other hunter in the woods. I wanted this to be my bird. As the turkey was getting closer and closer to me, I suddenly was able to see him in the clearing in front of me, and I was talking to myself in a whisper, "Come on baby, come a little bit closer." When I said that, I would have a clear shot, and I quickly stood up and took a shot at him, and the next thing I knew, the bird went down. I excitedly ran to the bird and laughed when I saw the devil lying on the ground dead. I bent down and picked up the bird by its talons and thought to myself what a great thing it would be to show my son or daughter, the thrill of the hunt. I had a great day. I learned that I would be a father, and I finally nailed that bird and would be hunting for months on end.

As the months passed, it looked like she was showing her motherhood shortly before we went to see the doctor and learned that it would be a boy. I really didn't care what it would be. I would love it just the same. I really don't like going for an ultrasound, because it takes away all the fun of guessing the baby's sex. The offices as long as I could remember gambled on an office pool on what sex it would be. And there would be no more of a surprise when you didn't know what it would be. We had an argument about it, but I finally gave into her, because she was into stuff like that.

My mom also took her side on the matter, so I was outvoted on the issue. I would have to go ahead with it, but after I went to the doctor and we had a discussion of what would be going on, that the event was just as exciting as if she was giving birth. I even found out that they could take a picture of it and would be able to give it to us for a keepsake. We agreed with them that we would very much like a picture of our baby.

As we left the office, I knew that I had a lot to do. I had an idea of a surprise for Sarah. I was planning to build our son his own room with the crib and everything. I had already gone to the architect, and the plans were all drawn up and we were ready to start the project. I couldn't wait to tell Sarah the good news. As we were driving back, I told her, "I need to stop here, and do you mind?" She noticed what the building was and said; "If you don't mind, I would like to go in there with you." I agreed that she should, and as we went into the building the person who would be our builder showed Sarah our plans for the next generation of Bradys. I might add that she was thrilled about the idea and gave me a big hug and said, "I'm very excited about this, honey. When did you decide to do this?" I figured that later on we would need something like this, because I figured later on that when the baby got older, he would like his own room." Sarah laughed and said, "I think that you're waiting to work on another Brady, aren't you?" As everyone laughed at me when my face turned red, I said, "I left myself wide open for that one, didn't I?" She replied, "You sure did."

At first, no one believed that he would be serious about the time of morning that he would wake up everybody.

There were a lot of unhappy faces all around me as the CO left for the evening. As everyone was getting ready for reverie, a trumpet blew taps in the distance, which meant sac time for us. As everyone started to fall asleep, it seemed that morning would come quickly and before you would know it.

There was a loud bang and a very loud voice yelling, "So you punks thought I would be joking about this, huh! Well, I got news for you punks, get up, and get up right now! Let's go! Move it! Come on! Stinky breaths! Let's go." After a while, he started to bang on the mop bucket. His partner would also join in, kicking a bucket around as well. One of our guys, however, didn't take him too seriously. No, it wasn't Charlie this time, it was Sam. The CO walked up to his bunk and said, "Would you want me to tuck you in, Seaman, or do you want me to sing you a lullaby?" And as the seaman turned and grunted, the CO turned the whole bunk over and the young seaman was on the floor. Everybody laughed as the young seaman was on his butt, looking up at the CO. The CO said, "You think that's funny? You punks aren't going to be laughing when I make you march ten miles with a heavy pack and make you run around the grinder a few laps. How about it? You are falling behind, and I hate being behind schedule. I'll show each and every one of you when I get a hold of you. And I bet that you will be up each and every time, or I will make your life a living nightmare!"

Finally, everyone was lined up outside and ready to march off to the chow hall. It seemed like it was miles before we reached the chow hall. But by the time we got there, everyone would be hungry and would be devouring everything in sight. As usual, the Navy would have everything lined up for you in the galley.

And you would have everything as usual for chow, such as eggs, bacon, toast, and grits, and pancakes that would be cooked to perfection. And pretty soon, after everyone finished eating, they were told to report outside the cafeteria.

Then after that, it would be time to settle in our new home for the next two months, as we were taught how to fix our bunks at the time. And pretty soon, as our CO instructed, time flew by, and it would be time for our lunch. As we finished making our bunks and as we lined up to march to lunch, who would've thought that we were already under his watchful eye? As we had a good lunch and as everyone gathered outside, we were instructed to march back to our barracks. When we arrived at our barracks, all of our bunks would be on the floor, because we failed to meet our majesty's inspection of all our bunks. For you see, this was part of our learning and instructions of discipline. Our CO walked in and said, "Well, I guess the punks didn't pay us any attention!" He would be talking to his partner, and as usual, his partner agreed with him. So again, we would be instructed one more time to make our bunks according to his instructions.

After a grueling lecture on how to make our bunks, our CO instructed us on how to fold and stow, as he put it, our clothes. And as we were lined up for this instruction, we found out how important it was to have an iron that we got at the PX. Everything we thought would be simple until you were up to the pants and shirt. It would be very important to get the wrinkles out of the shirt and pants, because they would be particular to see that you pay attention. If you didn't, you would not make the grade.

I thought that I had grasped the idea of folding and stowing the clothes but when we came back from lunch, we found all our clothes all over the floor. One's clothes would be mixed up with the other person's, even his underwear. Pretty soon, everyone would have no respect for our CO and would have dreams about how they would do away with him. In fact, one of our guys fell apart at the seams and he didn't make it. He would try to go AWOL and that would be a no-no in the Navy. I, however, wouldn't give up, and I wanted to prove to them that I wouldn't give them any trouble or complain at all. I would be bound and determined that I could take anything that they could dish out.

However, there was a surprise test. As soon as we were out of our bunks and getting ready for the next test, our CO said, "Now, let me tell you that I'm gaining respect for you people, and you better not let me down. So far, you have adjusted real well to our way of life here, and the time we spend getting to know each other has not been easy. I know this for a fact. This week, not only will you be going through with your physical training but you will also be going through the chamber. For you folks who don't know what I'm talking about you will find out soon enough. Also, after we report and get done with the chamber, you will report to the firing range. We will be spending a lot of time learning our weapons this week. In fact, this week we will be competing in and winning our firearms competition. If one of you goes away with a ribbon and medal, I would be ever so grateful, and not only that, you are going to become my personal yeoman. You will be in charge of the filing of our records and do other office duties. I hope that you will make it. Good luck and good hunting."

As the competition began, one of the CO's people was looking at me, and he began to whistle, impressed with my shooting capability. And s he walked off, I couldn't help but wear a big smile on my face, because, I knew that I would be the best shot. Every time I had a gun in my hand, I would hit a bull's-eye. The other CO walked towards my CO and said, "You ought to pay attention to the Brady fella that's over there shooting. He will win this competition with no problem, and I think that if we were at war, I would feel sorry for the enemy." The CO smiled and thanked him for the information and said, "I think that there would be no problem with him, because if he's from South Carolina, I feel that those people live in the woods and would have no problem in the other tests." The head CO said, "I hope you're right."

After the shooting competition, I was urged to make myself known and report to the CO. I told him that I would be there immediately. And as I ran to the office and checked myself to make sure everything was in tiptop shape, I remembered that I should knock real hard, and I did to acknowledge that I was reporting in very loudly as well. And then he responded, "Come in!" As I walked in very fast, I said, "Scott Brady reporting as ordered, sir!" The CO said, "At ease. I'm here to tell you, Scott, that I'm pretty damn impressed with you and your record around here. You're doing pretty good, and you did win the shooting competition. However, you have a long way to go. You have the maritime test, naval history, and last but not least, the reading test, and I hope that you are going to measure up for the task. However, you did win the shooting competition, and you passed the obstacle course, so you are getting there. Congratulations, yeoman." As I stood there, I didn't know how to reacted, because if I reacted in front of him, I felt he would punish me for being proud of myself. But I couldn't wait to write to my parents. They would be so proud of the fact that I was doing so well in the military. I knew that my father, being a WWII veteran, knew that it would be my destiny to be a military man.

As I stepped out of the office, I then reacted by saying, "Yeah hoo!" And on the other side of the door, the CO said, "I know, be proud of yourself son, you deserve it"

As I entered the office on the third week to start my duties as yeoman, the guys congratulated me for winning the shooting competition so that life for them would be made a lot easier. I thanked them and shook their hands and walked off to start my duties. The next week rolled around, and it would be survival. You would be teamed up with another guy, and you would be dropped off into the woods for a week, and you must find your way back to the base. They would weigh each person to see that they would lose weight, or be the same weight, or even gain weight. If you stayed the same weight or gained weight, you were bound to pass the completion.

As the weeks rolled on, time would go rapidly, and all of a sudden, it was "Hell Week," and believe you me, that was what it was. For some reason, as we were told to get up, it just seemed to me, that somehow it seemed earlier than usual. Pretty soon, I found out that I would be right. When we rolled out of our bunks, we would be in nothing but our Skivvies and a T-shirt. As the CO strolled in, we would find ourselves on the floor doing pushups and exercises that would go on through the night. By the end of the next day, none of us were on speaking terms. As the days went by, I noticed we were a well-oiled machine, and I felt that we were becoming a unit sure enough. I felt as though that I was beginning to understand the true meaning of the military, and the true word was teamwork. And as I began to understand this, I knew in my heart that I would be able to make it. I think that was the purpose of "Hell Week." By the time the next evening rolled around, our guys were completely exhausted. But I would be pretty excited about our next phase of training because it would involve firing our weapons that we would receive that week, even though, our CO didn't think that we would measure up to the task. Little did he know that I was trained with my father to hunt, and that I was raised to know how to handle handguns. After this, I knew that I would make the rest of the training, because most of the time, we learned about our weapons. We learned how to take it apart and put it back together blindfolded. We learned to sleep with our weapons, to "marry" our weapons. For the next week, we were on a "honeymoon" with our weapons. This is how I looked at it. I couldn't wait to get to the firing range. But first, the guys and I would have to go through a series of test: swimming, reading, and maritime history.

After we were weighed, all of us loaded into the truck for transport in to the woods. My partner and I entered the woods with only a knife and the clothes on our backs. I told him, "Hey, Phil, the first thing I would suggest that we do is to look for a spot where there would be water, and with all the vegetation around, I think that there should be water somewhere." Phil nodded in agreement and said, "What about heading towards the sun and see where it leads us?" I agreed, and so we walked through the woods, and sure enough, we started to hear water. We were getting pretty thirsty right about then. I looked around for any signs that the water was safe, but I noticed a type of sewage pipe and that waste was dripping into the water, and I said, "Hey Phil, I hate to burst your bubble, but I think that the water is unsafe, and I think we need to make a fire and boil the water to kill the bacteria that might be in the water." He agreed with me, and we started scurrying about, looking for branches and twigs for building a fire.

Going through our area, I noticed that there were some wild blueberries growing on the vine. I started to pick them, and Phil started building a fire, using his magnifier to reflect the sun off the glass and create enough heat to start the leaves burning and as he blew into the twigs and the branches, a fire started going.

He started to notice that I was separated from him, and he started to look for me, but I was not for off, and when he called me, I returned the favor to let him know that I was nearby. I walked back towards his voice and had my helmet off with a bunch of wild berries, and Phil said, "You must know your stuff in the woods; you already have supper. What else, sir?" I smiled and said, "I think that we need to build a shelter for the night. You never know when it may rain during the night, and I tell you what, if you take care of building a roof over our heads, I will call this dessert and try to get us a rabbit dinner." Phil was glad to take me up on my recommendation to set a snare for us to have rabbit stew. God, I felt like I would be Elmer Fudd in one of those Looney Tunes films.

And as luck would have it, we got lucky and snared a pretty large hare, which would feed both of us. Phil and I decided that we should have the berries and hare for a good supper because neither of us were really very hungry for lunch. But as I was thinking about that idea, I told him that we had no way of keeping the meat cold enough to last that long, and that if we didn't eat it right away, we could wind up in trouble over bad food. The berries didn't concern me, so we decided that we could have the meat for lunch and the berries for a light supper.

We ate a very hearty meal that would have been good enough for any restaurant in my home town of Charleston. We had our bellies full, and we had our shelter made for the night. We thought that we were all set until we heard the rumbling of thunder, and that meant only one thing: rain was on the way. We began to back ourselves into our manmade shelters and hoped for the best, that we wouldn't get too wet. However, we couldn't do anything about the wet ground, and we found it hard to sleep that night. As we lay there staring at one another, contemplating about the fix that we were in, it became very dangerous for us as a bolt of lightning came forth and split a nearby tree down the middle. As you know, when that bolt of lightning hit, we both jumped like cats that were nailed by a rocking chair. We hoped the rain would pass quickly.

However, a thought came across my mind. I took off my helmet and caught the rainwater, as it fell hard around us. Phil caught on as well and did the same, and when the helmet became full, we emptied the helmet into our canteens.

As we survived, from day to day, we were confident that with teamwork, we would make this thing, and with plenty of food such as frogs, lizards, roots, and berries, and with plenty of water that we were able to find, the two weeks went by pretty quickly. I won't ever forget the last day, for we had entered a part of the wetlands that would be without the vegetation we needed in order for us to start a fire. After using a long stick for a fishing rod and a piece of string from our jackets, and a using a safety hook from my jacket as well, I was able to catch us a couple of fish for a good last meal on our journey. Phil was so hungry looking at those two fish flapping on the ground that the thought of eating them raw seemed like a good idea, but I, on the other hand, didn't like the idea of doing that to my body. As I looked around, Phil was watching me, and he said, "What are you doing?" I'm all for the digging in right now, according to the way my stomach is growling." I told him like he didn't know what I meant, which he didn't. As I looked around, after cleaning the fish, I said, "Well, here is what I have been looking for." I took a handful of mud and started packing our meal in a big mud ball." And I told him, "Watch and learn from a South Carolina graduate. A fighting Gamecock will not be eating raw fish. As you will notice, my young friend, the sun is a beautiful planet, which keeps us warm all spring and summer, and when you have the heat and humidity like it is today, the mud, which I'm packing around my fish, will be hard in a short amount of time when I put it in a spot with no shade, such as right here for example. As one cooks, I'll get another ready to broil in the sun." Phil said, "How long will it take to be ready?" I told him, "Well, with the hot sun, I think that it would be ready in a couple of hours."

And sure enough, he was soon enjoying a hot fish dinner, and as predicted, the mud baked to a hard ball, and when I opened them up, the fish were hot and steamy on the inside. Phil said, "Let me at those things. I'm hungry enough to eat worms." And as we sat down, both of us had a great meal, for we were getting close to the pick-up point and nearing the highway.

My Dad, who was very happy, yelled out with excitement as he started out a new adventure with someone new. He would be ever go grateful to my aunt for doing this for him, and while celebrating, said to Lydia, laughing, "You made me a happy man, Lydia, and I will pick you up around 8:00 p.m. tonight, if that would be all right with you?" Lydia said, "That would be all right Cecile, and I look forward to meeting you. I hope it would be all right for me to meet your son one day?" My Dad smiled and said," Why it would be very much okay. My son has been doing without any female company for a long time as well. His grieving over his mother has been going on for a long time, and maybe if you two connect, I think that he'll be all right too."

Later that day, I finally came in from work, and when I came in, something grabbed me out the blue and started hugging me. My Dad said, as he let me down, "How are you today, my boy?" As he took me by surprise, I said, "What happened Dad? Did you win the lottery or something, and if so how about you split it with me so I can retire too?" My Dad laughed and said, "No, my boy, I met someone, and pretty soon, if everything worked works out right, I won't be lonely no more."

As I took the news of his new romance in, I said, "Well, how well do you know this girl, Dad? Is she honest? Are you sure that she won't take advantage of you?" As I said that, Dad didn't seem to take it very well and said, "Well, I thought you would be happy for your old man, but I see that you have some concerns." I told my dad, "I'm happy for you, Dad, but you know that when you took me into the family, I have always been the black sheep of the family, and you know it." My dad who looked shocked about what I said came back with, "You know the family doesn't feel that way about you." I told him, "Well, I guess you don't remember the conflict with my mother, my grandmother, and my stingy uncle over a stupid Christmas gift that I wanted, and that he didn't want to buy me anything, now don't you?" I continued. "All I need is for you to get married and to find out that the family you might be getting into would not accept me either." My dad said, "Well I don't think you have to worry about Lydia. I think that she will accept you with open arms, once she gets to know you."

My dad said, "Well Doc, I guess you leave me no choice, but to quit these things that I love so dearly even more than my girlfriend or my son." The doctor shook his head and said, "you really have to quit, or I'm warning you right now, you will die, and that's no to say that you really don't have a chance to survive this operation." My dad, who now is trying to listen, and for the first time said, "If you're trying to scare me, it's working, because you see, I do want to live a long life, and I want to make up with Lydia. You see Doc, I thought that I loved cigarettes more than her, but I thought wrong, I will quit these things, Doc, and I'll do what you say and follow your advice."

The doctor looked pessimistic at first and said, "Well then Mr. Brady, give me those things right now, and I will believe you." My dad looked at him and said, "Oh come on, Doc, you're putting me in a good spot." The doctor smiled and said, "Well, put up or shut up then. Give them to me right now. My dad, quite reluctantly, gave him all the cigarettes that he had." The doctor grinned, after he won the war and said, "Now, it's going to be hard for you the rest of the way because we are going to be putting you on a special diet. Also, you will have surgery in a month. I want you to go to the nurse up front and let her schedule your surgery, and may we pray that you get better."

My dad thanked him for everything that he was doing to help him, and naturally, the doctor exclaimed that it was a hard thing that he had to do, but it would be the only way to make him see the light. As dad went up to the nurse and scheduled the heart operation. He thought to himself that he needed to tell Lydia everything about what happened and what would happen.

It would be time that he would have to go through the hardest thing in his life. First, you had to go to this class to learn what kind of procedure it is and what kind of hard drugs that he would be taking during and after the surgery. This would be a week or two before the surgery. After he was prepared for what was to come, the day of the surgery would be stressful enough for dad, but for me and Lydia it would be awful. After hearing about this, I came down and helped the family out as well.

After Dad pulled into the drive, I walked out to greet him. He immediately rushed into the house and told me "Son, I have something important to tell you."

It seems that the doctor had told my dad, "Yeah, I think that would be wise, if you want to live a long time with Lydia. You should give those things up." My dad told me, "I don't know if I can do that, son. I have been smoking and drinking for so long. That I don't know if I ever will quit." I told him, "Well, maybe you don't love me or Lydia like you say you do, or else you would quit cold turkey, and you would never miss them." My dad said, "Well, I have an appointment with Dr. Wrench tomorrow morning, and he told me that he wanted to run several tests on me to see what's wrong."

I knew that he wouldn't give me a straight answer on the quitting issue, so I told him, "Dad you're going to have to face it sooner or later. You will have to give up those things, especially if you want to have a life with Lydia." He didn't say anything after that. It seems like that when a person is involved with that type of habit, they don't want to even try to quit, even if it means that they may die.

That morning, he rushed off to see Dr. Wrench, and while waiting, Lydia said, "I hope that you have given consideration to quitting those damn cigarettes, Cecile?" Dad looked at her as if to say, *The hell with you.* Lydia said, "I know you pretty good, and I'm here to tell you, Cecil, that if you want to spend a lifetime with me, you will quit." My dad told her, "If that is the way you feel, maybe you need to go right now, because life is too short to be cautious about everything, and I will not quit." After hearing this, she said, "Well then maybe you don't love me anymore, and you love those things even more, so therefore Cecil, I'm telling you goodbye for good."

Dr. Wrench walked in after the exchange and told dad, "Well, Mr. Brady, I'm going to tell you some bad news that I always hate to tell, and that is if you don't give up that nasty habit, you are going to die. I'm also going to tell you that it is imperative, that you have a four-way bypass, because all of the arteries in your heart are a hundred percent blocked, and if you don't have surgery, you will die."

When he finally became so weak that he could not respond back to anything, I went to the phone and called the EMS and told them what happened, and the dispatcher, told me to stand by, because he would be sending some help. Sure enough, I started to hear a knock at the door, and I immediately opened the door to let them in.

The EMS worker looked at me and said, "How long has this been going on?" I told him, "It's been going on for a long time. While he was still awake, he told me not to call you guys." The EMS worker said, "Well, I hope we can get him to the emergency room in time, because it doesn't look very good." He continued to say, "In fact, he is losing all body fluids from all kinds of angles here, and we need to get him there fast." I told him, "I agree with you, but like I told you, I couldn't do anything at the time while he was still conscious."

The EMS worker finally said, "I see your point of view; you still respect your dad and try to obey him. "I nodded my head as he rolled Dad to the back of the ambulance, and as they drove off, I decided that his sister should know about the emergency situation at once. I picked up the phone and called her number, and then there was a voice on the other end, "Hello, who is this?" I noticed that her voice was like she had just woken up, and I was afraid she was going to let me have it. But I said, "Hey, this is your favorite nephew. I didn't mean to call you so late, but I just wanted to let you know that something awful happened to Dad, and he is on the way to the hospital, and it look pretty serious right now." She was silent for a few minutes and said, "I'm sorry to hear that, but there is nothing I can do for you right now." I'm down here in Florida, and I'm not feeling very well myself." I told her, "I can understand that in these situations you feel helpless to do anything, but I still thought that it would be important for you to know." She took a moment to come back to me and said, "Well, let me go. I need to go back to sleep." I hung up the phone after I told her goodbye, and all of a sudden, I felt all alone with nowhere to go. All I could do then was wait, but when my dad comes back, if he makes it, I'd make sure he would be comfortable.

It would be murder waiting in the waiting room, as dad was laid out. I was having a bad feeling that he would not make it, especially when they told me that they would have to take a buzz saw and cut into the chest bone in order to get to the heart muscle. It sounded as scary as it could be, and I was showing a lot of stress, worrying about my dad. After a while, the doctor finally came into view and said, "It was touch and go there for a while, but I think that he will be all right. You can go see him only for a few minutes. Then I would suggest that you go home and get some rest, because I know that you had to wait for a long time and that it would be stressful on anybody to wait for this long." After hearing the news, we decided that it would be best for me to go home and get something to eat and get a good night's rest. When the doctor left, we went to the area where Dad was at. When we came to his bedside, it was scary, as he lay there cold and stiff as can be. It was if he were really dead. After seeing that, I started to cry as if I were grieving. I was scared that that was it.

After getting home, I was quiet as a mouse on Christmas Eve waiting on Santa Clause. My aunt was quiet too. She tried to break the silence by asking me what I wanted to eat. I told her, "Did you feel his body? It was so cold. I thought that he was dead." She said, "Well if you remember, the nurse instructing the class said that he would be like that for a good while, and that it may take days for him to recover. I believe that it would be normal to feel the way you do, but that you should not have anything to worry about." I told her, "I guess you're right, but I can't stop thinking that his body was so cold; it scares me." She urged me again, "Hey, don't worry about it. It will be all right. Okay, Scott? Now, what do you want to eat? You really need to eat something." I told her, "You know what? I really could go for a Bessinger's basket, and I have a barbeque attack." My Aunt said, "You know what? That sounds like a good idea. I think I will have the same."

Luckily, Dad came through everything just fine. He also gave those ugly things up as well. Unfortunately, after a period of time, Dad never really gained any strength to amount to anything. Also, he has picked up something known as congestive heart failure. Every few days, his body swells up with fluid, and he has to report to the hospital. And for a short time, he went blind for a while and completely lost his sight in one eye and gained all of his sight back in the other. Lydia, however, does not see Dad anymore, because it breaks her heart to see him suffer. But one must realize that when you are his age and poor in health, you are not going to be leaping tall buildings in a single bound. When a person gets in this state of life, it seems that the whole world is against you, and that you don't have anything in life to live for. It seems like it's just a matter of time. I had to look at myself too and wonder where the time went, because I'm getting to the ripe old age of fifty now.

Where has time gone? I have always wondered. That is why whenever I see Dad, I always try to do the right thing and help him as much as possible. Since the poor man can never walk, even a few inches, I needed to be there to give a helping hand. I guess, that's because he is family, and kin will look after kin.

So, I decided that I would stay with him and look after things such as paying bills, cleaning the house, and getting anything he wished or desired. I, however, didn't know what kind of rough road lay ahead. Also, I didn't know that it would be a 24-hour job. I somehow needed to work things out, or I would never get any sleep. Some nights, I wouldn't be able to rest well until 3:00 in the morning.

But I have to keep going, I would say to myself. After getting things for him, I also had to wash the linen, the clothes, and the cleaning of the house. And after all that, he would call me out of bed for different things, all night long, until he would be completely exhausted by early the next morning.

During these difficult times ahead, it seemed that it would be a test of will between my dad and me. There would be a lot of fighting and snapping at each other. And during these times, I would be thinking that we needed to be a team instead of at each other's throats. I know that it would be hard on him because he had to plan everything, and that I'm never home to help him that much, because I would always be on the job. I guess that was because if my opinion didn't count and since I was considered the black sheep of the family, the best I could do for myself would be to go to work and just take the time off when I would be needed most during and after the funeral, a time in which you would have to plan the relatives that would be staying at the house. We had to make arrangements, so that everyone would be comfortable with the sleeping arrangements. I hope that he would let me help with making sure that our group would have plenty to drink and eat at the ceremony. After all, I hoped that he didn't think that I was the black sheep of the family.

Well, it was the day of the funeral, and it was a sad time for us, as we were the center of attention of the family. They were wearing the black, and the preacher was saying a beautiful sermon over mom. Dad and I were in tears, as the preacher came to our section and shook our hands and said, "May God be with both of you, my sons." We both thanked him for a wonderful sermon and told him that we would be in church on Sunday.

As we gathered at the house, everyone was talking and doing some catching up, and during all this, my dad came to me as I was talking to Uncle Herman and I told him, "Excuse me, but I have a phone call to get to." My uncle nodded in agreement, so I went to answer the phone. I said, "Hello, who's this please?" The voice on the other end said, "Hey! This is your boss, and I need you to work tonight, Scott. The fellow who was supposed to take your place at this time quit, and I really need you." I told him, "I hope you know you are asking a lot, and that I have roomful of people here." The boss said, "I know that, but I really need you to come in tonight." I told him, "Let me tell you something, I hope you know that you owe me a big one and make it worth my while." So I decided that I would come in, and I knew that the proper thing would be for me to hang up the phone and make my apologies to our guests. I went to the other room to change into my work clothes, and I reported to work.

"I may have to apologize now, in case I make too much of a pig of myself." Lydia and her daughter both laughed as I said that, and Lydia told Dad, "Cecil, I never could imagine how charming your son is." As they were just finishing setting the table, and as they were getting ready to sit down I sad, "Here let me help you lovely ladies to your chair. They both looked at each other as if they were impressed by my actions. My dad said, "My, but doesn't all this looks scrumptious." Lydia said, "Why thank you Cecil! Really, it wasn't any kind of trouble to fix you boys a nice home cooked meal for a change." Both my father and I were in agreement that it was a nice thing for her to do, and that we appreciated everything she had done for us.

As the evening went on, Lydia said, "Well, Scott, your dad told me that you were in the military for quite a while, is that true?" I responded to her, "Yes ma'am, I was in there for a hitch, and I just got tired of it and all the traveling that came to be part of the territory." Lydia said, "What kind of rank did you have when you left?" I told her, "I was a petty officer third class, ma'am." Lydia said, "I guess it would be hard to make any friends with such a lifestyle."

I told her, "Yes ma'am, I don't know if my dad told you or not, but at one time I was married to a beautiful lady, and she gave me a beautiful boy, but due to the fact that I was always be putting my life on the line for my county, she decided to divorce me and take my kid away from me. To this day, I don't know where they are, as she hasn't made any effort to contact me, or let my kid even call me or let me know whether he is happy or not. She may have poisoned his mind against me by now." Lydia said, "I think that was awful of her to do that to you Scott, because I think you're a nice guy." I simply responded, "Why, thank you, ma'am."

When they finally met at the restaurant, Lydia stood up to show Dad where she was sitting as she noticed him coming into the place. The restaurant was by the river, known in our neck of the woods as the Cooper River. It was romantic to be sitting at the table with a view of the river beside you. Lydia said, "Well, how are you today, Cecil?" My dad said, "May I say my dear, being with you has been the bright spot of my evening." Lydia laughed and said, "Well, you certainly do know how to impress a lady, Cecil." My dad replied, "Well, that's my job, honey, to make your every wish come true." Lydia said, "Oh my, you better not promise too much, Cecil. I may take you up on that offer." My dad said, "You really mean that, Lydia?" My assumption would be right. I thought that Dad was rushing into something and hoping a lot more would happen than a casual date. And the conversation continued. "Cecil, I don't know what to say. You treat me like a queen and show me more respect than most men I have dated have done, except for my husband, who has been gone for all these years." My dad said, "Well, Lydia, I feel the same way about you, and hopefully I have impressed you enough, that I would be able to spend the night with you," Lydia thought for a moment and said, "Cecil, we have just met, and I don't really want to say yes right now." As she continued, "You know I like you and all, and for right now, all I want to be is friends. But give me a little time. I may grow fonder of you, and sometime later I may take you up on that tempting offer." My dad, who was looking disappointed at this time, said, "I can understand what you're saying, but think about this. Think about how lonely you've been all these years, every night without someone by your side to keep you company, and to hold you and to love you."

As dad said this, Lydia had a look on her face that he could be right. But it still stands, she thought to herself, that it wouldn't be very respectful of her if she went to bed with anyone, and besides, her daughter wouldn't understand this at all if she would come in the door with a strange man at her side. She finally came back and said. "Cecil, I hope you know that what I'm about to tell you is something most men don't want to hear, and that is I have a daughter, who is living with me right now, and I hope that you can understand how it would look if I came home with you right now."

My dad said, "Well, that came out of the blue, because my sister didn't mention anything about you having a daughter, but when she said that you were a widow for so many years, I should have known that you might have children." Lydia said, "I told your sister not to mention that, because I wanted to be the one to tell you." She continued, "I hope that you're not turned off by the fact that I have a daughter?" My dad thought for a moment and said, "Well, no, because I thought that by the way you talked on the phone and by the way you were acting when I told you I had a son." Lydia said, "I hope that you forgive me for that, because I should have known that you raised your son to respect people and their feelings, especially since you told me that Scott was in the military. I know now that I acted foolishly, and I hope you will forgive me."

My dad said, "I hope that you can call it even, and I apologize for my actions as well." Lydia said, "Well, how about we both forget it, and forget that it ever happened." My dad agreed and blew a sigh of relief. My dad thought that he blew it there for a minute, but as luck would turn out, he was grateful that both of them came to an agreement that they would keep in contact with each other and that they would go out more. Lydia also said, "I also hope that your son and I can meet, and I hope you can arrange it soon." My dad said, "My son would be glad to meet you; all we have to do is to arrange it." Lydia said, "Well, why don't we have dinner at my place on Friday night or any night that he would be off, and we go on from there and see how it works out?" As it turned out, my dad still had a delightful evening, and he was confident that everything would be fine between us. I think that his goal all along was to make us a family unit again, and that later on, maybe marriage wouldn't be out of the question." My dad was just tired of being lonely, but I had a feeling that he just shouldn't rush into this thing.

For a long time there after that evening, everyone was getting along really well. We would be having a lot more dinners after that, and one day, she decided that she wanted to travel with dad and see some of our great country, and I told Dad that I thought that would be great for him and her to travel around together. I also thought that it would give them time to even fall in love with each other that much more. My dad told me, "You like her now, don't you?" I told my dad, "Yes, sir, I think I do." My dad smiled, gave me a hug, and said, "Thank you, Scott, for helping me during this time of need. I appreciate everything that you have done for me." I told him, "It's my pleasure, Pop, but I just want to make sure that you're happy." My dad, at that point, assured me that he was happy and that he was thinking very seriously about getting married." I told him, "Dad, I don't think that it would be a good time to do that." He then asked me, "Why? I thought that you liked her." Well, Pop, you have to think about each other's income. If you marry her, one of your checks would be gone out the window." He looked at me and said, "You know, son, I think you are right on that one, maybe it would be a good idea to live together." I agreed with him on that point, and I told him that there would be no objection from me."

During their trip out of town, I received a phone call shortly after they were gone. I would say that it was two days into their trip when I received the call. I picked up the phone and heard, "Scott, this is Lydia. I just wanted to let you know that you father is in the hospital with chest pains, and that it looks like he has had a heart attack." All of a sudden, I think that hearing the news came as a shock. I asked her after a long pause, "Is he all right? And what are the doctors doing for him?" She told me, "Right now, the doctors think that after they get him stabilized that he should see a heart specialist back home, and that's what we are waiting on now, and as soon as we can, we are going home." I told her, "Well, keep me posted on what is going on, and by the way, I wish that you would get him to quit smoking, I have told him and fought with him for a long time that those things were bad for him." She told me, "Yes, Scott, I agree with you. I also think that these cigarettes are also bad." As I hung up the phone, I was thinking to myself, that this was a true test of me. Maybe, it's going to come to a point that I am going to have to take care of him now, and he will need me. I decided that I would do all that I could to take care of him.

After we landed, a bus picked us up at the Orlando Airport, and it transported the boots, as we were called, to the base for basic training. As we got off the bus, there was a gentleman to greet us, and he was not very pleasant. His name was Petty Officer Tom Burding, and he was a rough customer to get along with for twelve weeks. As we started off the bus, he would say, "All right troops, look alive. Come on, we haven't got all day! We need to get you guys settled in for the night, and believe you me, gentlemen, you better take advantage of your beauty sleep, you ugly pukes, because believe me you are going to have a full day tomorrow." It was hard to believe that I was there and sure enough you have one in every crowd. There is always a smart one, who has to learn the hard way. He would always be smiling in the ranks, and you don't do those things. When our CO came to where he was at, he would say, "Well, well, what are you so happy about? You better get that smile off your face, puke!" The boy just didn't know who he was messing with. Our CO came back to where he was and said, 'Well you must think that there is something funny. Get down and give me fifty pushups, and I mean right now, mister. Get a move on now!" And when he said that, the boy immediately went down on all fours and started to do his punishment for disobedience. The CO said, "Listen, you pukes. I will be for the next twelve weeks your momma and your papa. We will not have you whining babies calling home for mommy and daddy while you're here. I repeat, I am your mamma and your poppa. Do I make myself clear, you pukes!" Everyone started to say, "Sir! Yes sir!" He started to laugh and say, "Now, you know that I am laughing because I can't hear a word you're saying, and therefore, to make sure that you know how to speak up, I must have everyone do fifty pushups." He walked a few steps, he turned around while we were laughing and thinking he was joking, he exclaimed, "Right now!" And when he gave the command to do so. We all dropped and began doing them to our disbelief.

I thought to myself that we were paying for our mistake of making our esteemed CO fall behind schedule. Finally, after a two hour wait in the hot sun, our CO finally appeared and said, "Well, I hope that you pukes had a good meal, because the next step is to go to the beauty shop, so that you ladies can get your hair done." So as we were ordered to line up for the next march, and as he said, "Forward march!" We started moving down the pave road, and again it seemed like it would go on and on. Finally, after reaching our destination, everyone would be totally exhausted. And sweat would be pouring off everyone. The CO said, "Well, when I get through with you punks, you are going to be in the greatest shape than anyone in this company. We are going to work day and night, until you are fighting Navy men." "And what do you say to that, gentlemen, as I use the term loosely!" Every one said in unison, "Sir, yes sir!" Okay, as I thought to myself, I always needed a haircut, and I could go for a trim. And again I thought he would be kidding about getting our heads shaved, so we arrived at the place where they gave your haircuts. Our names were called out, and finally it was my turn. As I sat down, I said, "Just take a little off the sides and the top and taper off to the back a little." And before I knew it, the barber smiled, and he took those shears and went from the front to the back. Before I knew it, I walked away, feeling a few pounds lighter.

After everyone gathered outside after their trim, rubbing their heads, never feeling as naked as they did before, we were again told to line up to pick up our own personal gear. Our CO said, "Well! You pukes look like gentleman now, and now it is time for everyone to get your gear and uniforms, so left face! Forward march!" And again, it seemed to take forever to get to the UPC as the Navy called it. And as we lined to pick up our gear, they would have our pants, shirts, shoes, and other gear lined up like a buffet table.

As our CO ordered us to go into the barracks, there was a lot of hustle and bustle as the new recruits were trying to get to know one another. All of the sudden, there was a loud and boisterous CO, who finally came in behind us. And he told us, "Shut up now, you puke heads.

I want to give you our itinerary for tomorrow morning, so if I were you, I would listen up, for tomorrow will be a very busy day. For instance, this isn't home by any means. Your mommy and daddy will not be getting you up at 8:00 a.m., so you will be off to school. Oh no! Our day will start at 4:30 in the morning, sharp! You will, and I repeat, you will be up and ready to roll out of your bunks. After you pukes get out of your bed, you children will proceed to chow; as you will note, Uncle Sam's Navy will feed and cloth you pukes for the next twelve weeks, and believe you me, it won't be any picnic. After chow, we will go to the barber shop, and we will give you pukes an old fashioned bald cut, and I will personally be there to enjoy each puke getting his head shaved. Another thing, after that, you will report to receive your uniform, while you are there, and other gear that you need for your stay here. You will also go to the PX where you will need to purchase, out of your vouchers, an iron to get those wrinkles off your clothes, and you will find it necessary to get you a notebook, because you will have to copy off this blackboard, a POD. And to you civilian pukes that means the plan of the day. Heed my warning. If you should have the desire to pay me a visit in my office—" All of a sudden, one of the new recruits was snickering, and the CO heard it and went to where he was and said, "Do you find this funny? Because I don't find you a bit funny. You will then proceed to give me a hundred pushups, and after that, you will stand in the corner like you were in grade school, and you will stay there all night long. Maybe this will cure your snickering problem. Do I make myself clear?" The young recruit, said, "Sir! Yes sir!" I didn't hear you seaman, what did you say?" The young recruit, whose name was Charles, said, "Sir! Yes Sir! The CO told the young man, "Okay, you may carry on, Seaman, and let this be a lesson to all of you. And another thing, as I was so rudely interrupted, you will knock loudly on this door, because if I don't hear you, I will make you do so many pushups, you will never forget to do so!" Do you understand? Sir! Yes Sir!"

The next phase, however, would be a little tough. It would be a test that I knew would be difficult, the naval history test. It would be the next thing on the list. I noticed that some of the questions were easy and some were not. I just hoped I could pass it and that I would enjoy liberty on the weekend. We all would go to Sea World. As I read each question, it seemed that passing this thing would be impossible. I would not be too sure of how I would do on this one, and that I would be nervous, again, like a cat with a room full of rocking chairs. As I finished, the instructor told everyone to report before revelry.

That evening, I was crossing my fingers, and I could feel the tension, as he would be reading each person's scores. When he finally reached me, I stood up and said, "Yes sir!" He looked at me in such a way led me to believe that I didn't do so well, but when he said, "Well, Mr. Brady, what have you got to say for yourself? Well, let's see what we have here. Your reading test score, 98; your maritime score, 98; you passed the swim test, and the survival test, and the infantry test. Well, it looks like congratulations are in order. Welcome to the United States Navy." I stood up and hollered, and as I did that, the rest of the company clapped their hands.

Later on, as I was packing my gear and getting ready for graduation, Phil walked up to me and said, "Well, it was nice knowing a fighting chicken such as yourself, and a smart one to." We both laughed and said, "Well, who's to say that a cornhusker and a chicken can't be friends." Phil laughed and said, "Where are you going to be stationed now?" I looked at him and said, "I want to follow in my dad's footsteps, and I would like to be in CID or Sid and help you guys get information from the enemy." Phil said, "Well good luck, you deserve it. Try to contact me. I think they are going to assign me to the Ronald Reagan." We both shook hands, and to this point, I have heard something from him every now and then.

I was glad to spend some time with my parents as we toured the town of Orlando. We saw all the sights at Disney World, and all the animals of Sea World. We were also there to see Shamu the whale do a lot of the stunts that made him famous. As we were leaving Disney, my mom and dad decided that they wanted to treat me to a dinner, so we picked out a restaurant and went to it.

At the restaurant my parents were greeted by the hostess, and she said, "My, who is this fine-looking young man?" My father said, "This is my son, young lady, and my son today is a full-fledged navy man. He just graduated from boot camp today." The young hostess smiled and gave me a hug and said, "I'm impressed, and how much longer will you be in town?" I told her, "I don't know, but I would be happy to escort you one night if you are free." She smiled and said, "I will make time, because you must be new in town, and I could show you a good time." I shook my head in agreement and asked her, "What time should I pick you up, tonight?" She smiled and said, "How about you wait a few minutes, because I get off soon and could join you and your family for dinner, and maybe we could go to the beach later." I told her, "I would be quite honored to go anywhere that you want to go, ma'am."

As everyone enjoyed a good meal and good conversation, the restaurant hostess, whose name I found out was Sarah, told me, "You don't know where you are going?" And as I hesitated, I noticed that the young lady was smitten with me. So I thought I would give her great news, and I told her I was going to be stationed in the Florida area, and that I was going to be sticking around for a while. After I said that, she was ecstatic and said, "You know, Scott, I'm glad that I bumped into you. Now we can see a lot of each other, can't we?" I told her that we could, and so therefore I would have my first romance with a beautiful woman. For a while we would see each other quit frequently, and things were going quite well, believe it or not. We seemed to be hitting it off, but all of a sudden, I was called into the office the next day and the CO said, "Mr. Brady, we have a new set of orders for you. You are going to report to your home town. I believe that you are from Charleston, aren't you?" I told him, "Yes sir, I am, but I'm enjoying staying here. I met someone who I love very much, and I want to stay here." The CO told me, "When you join this man's Navy son, you have to go where you are told and are needed, and you are needed home." I humbly agreed, and I knew that in my heart that if I wanted to succeed in this man's Navy, I had to take the bad with the good, and somehow I would have to tell Sarah the bad news when I got off, I walked back to the desk and picked up the phone to call her. She answered the phone, "Hello," I said, "Sarah, I need to tell you something important, and it is not good news." She said, "What do you mean? Did I do anything wrong or hurt your feelings in any way? I want to apologize to you right now because I love you Scott Brady, and don't you forget that." I smiled and said, "No, it's nothing you've done. You are a beautiful, sensuous woman, and I love you desperately, but the news I have for you is that I have been transferred to Charleston, SC. I'm going to be head of security there." She told me, "Well, whatever it is, I want to go with you." I was so pleased to hear those words, as they rolled out of her mouth. I told her, "You make me the happiest man in the world, and I would be honored if you would have dinner with me." She agreed and I knew that I would have a lot to do on this day.

And as I said that, her jaw dropped like an anchor off an aircraft carrier, and then I said, "Hey, I'm serious. You told me that you're in love with me, didn't you?" She paused and said, "Well, yeah? But marriage, Scott? You know how to take a girl off her feet." I told her, "That doesn't answer my question. Will you marry me?" She replied, "Scott Brady, I would be proud and honored to marry you twenty times over, so yes! Yes!" I laughed and was pleased as punch that she agreed to marry me, and I told her, "You know I have to let my mom and dad know, and all my friends. We have to get married in my hometown. You have made me a happy man. I have so many things to do and plan. Oh! I mean plan out. I'm so nervous. Look at me, I'm shaking with excitement." She replied, "Well, how about dinner?" After thinking about it, I said, "I have so many things to do. Can I take a rain check, because, my darling, we will have a lifetime of dinners together." She laughed, as she watched me make a fool of myself, like I was a kid again.

As I went back to my apartment, I immediately called my mom. When she answered the phone, I said, "Hey Mom, I have some good news for you. I'm getting married." My mom, said, "what did you say, son? I thought I heard you say that you are getting married?" I replied, "That's right, Mom. I'm getting married. You remember Sarah, the nice hostess at the restaurant where we had dinner together? After you left, we became very close, and now we are at this juncture, and Mom, I have some more good news." My mom said, "I don't know if my heart can stand any more of this. What else, son?" I replied, "Hang on. I didn't want to come home at this point, but I am coming home to be head of security at the base, and I'm going to be Dad's boss." My mom said, "You're kidding?" I then said laughing, "That's right, Mom. I'm coming home with your new daughter-in-law, and get used to the idea that I'm dad's boss." My mother, who screamed with delight, shouted out to my dad, who I heard in the background, ecstatic as well. And as the end of the day drew near, it seemed hard to sleep, but I knew that everything would work out, and how I knew that I would have a couple of parents that seemed to be happy for me as well.

As you may recall, I had already been to a recruiter to see about enlisting for the Navy. I was getting tired of the same old hassle of getting up during the day to get back to work each night and putting up with people that you meet on the job each night. I don't know about you, but I had a hard road to hold. Getting shot was no fun, and putting my life on the line wouldn't be fun either. I was talking to the recruiter and he was giving me the details of the advantage of joining the military, a steady career that I would enjoy almost my lifetime, also the travel and the places that I would see and do. I would see the world and in its entire splendor. I was thrilled as he sweet talked me into signing up. I had a six month delayed entry program in which I would be able to convince my mom that it was time for me to leave the nest and to seek out my destiny. I hoped to convince her that even though I knew she loved me and didn't want me to go, that it would be the best thing overall. Even though, I would be putting my life in jeopardy, it still would give me a better future and pay scale. Also, I wouldn't have to worry about that ordeal until there was a war, and I didn't see that happening for a long time to come. Even though we had Russia to deal with, I knew that we had a great president at the time to deal with the situation. He was one of my heroes, and his name was Ronald Reagan. I have always been a fan of his since I was a little kid. And I knew that his policies would keep me safe. One day when I was home, the letter finally came in the mail. My mom came into the room and confronted me, saying, "What is this letter about? And when did you see these people?" I told my mom, "Hey Mom, you see it's like this. I want to join the military, because it is a good future, and I think that I could make it my career. I want to do this, Mom, and I hope that you can understand where I'm coming from. I don't like what I'm doing. I'm tired of getting up and going to work at ok/

.ok-.-----

-

night, so I hope that you can understand also. I'm tired of dealing with the people, and I'm also tired of getting shot at or fighting the bad guy and protecting money that doesn't even belong to me and also getting very little of it to boot." My mom was shocked that I presented such a good case about why I should go. She didn't even want to argue with me. All she could say was "Well, I hope that they treat you all right and that you'll be safe. But as a mother, may I tell you I'm going to worry about you, and you better write to us and call us whenever yo can." I told her, "I will write to you, Mom, and don't worry, I don't think that there will be a war for a long time. This will give me a chance to experience going to different places and seeing the wonders of the world." I thought that it went very well, and even my father took me to the side and said, "You know, I talked to your mother, and we had a heck of an argument as I tried to convince her that it would be a good thing for you to enlist, because it didn't hurt at all. I also tried to explain to her that the army would train you to be a responsible young man and to be all that you can be. But don't put me in the middle of an argument again."

So that Monday morning, I decided to tell of him about my new career. He came in as usual at 7:00 a.m., and he came out of his own personal wrecker that he would drive home in. He reached out to the office door, and when the car pulled into the station for service, he told me to go out there and take care of it. And as I did, he noticed that it would be one of his regular lady customers. As I asked her what she would have today, she told me, "Good morning, I would like a fill up, and please check under the hood." I told her that I would be glad to, so as I began to put the nozzle in the tank, he, Mr. Radcliff, started a conversation with her and said the usual stuff, kind of picking on her. They would laugh and joke for a while, and while I was under the hood checking things out, he told her to hold on while he would check and see how I was coming along. She told him, "I appreciate the fine job that Scott is doing, and that he has always treated me nice, and that I love coming to your station. The boss smiled and said, "Yes ma'am, we sure do appreciate your business." As she thanked him, he was walking toward the hood and was watching me as I was about to check the transmission oil for her. I yelled out for her to cut the engine on so that I could check her oil, and she nodded her head in agreement.

As the motor was running, the boss said, "How about checking her air filter? And kind of stomp on it so that it looks like she needs a new one. Come on, she would buy one." I politely put the stick in her transmission, and told her that it would be all right. I didn't do what he asked me to do. I went as far as checking the filter, but I didn't do as he told me to about stomping on it. After she drove off, I said, "Look here. I'm not one of your thieves, and I don't steal from the customers. You have the wrong person, and I don't think I'm going to work here anymore." And as I walked off the job, he was standing there, almost as if he was a statue in the park or something.

That was the last straw that broke the camel's back. I told the boss, "I had a tough night. I'm soaked to the bone, and I need to get home." The boss regained his focus and nodded his head like, *Sure, go ahead home.* I went back to the car, got in and took off for home. I drove through all the debris left from the storm.

As I pulled into the drive of my home, I noticed that there was no damage to my home, and I was so glad. The only thing that I could think of was my bed. It would be the finest thing for me at that moment, and I didn't think anything in the world could hold me back from it either. But I had to wonder what the night would bring for me.

Well, it would be quite for the next few nights, and I would be wondering how long it would last. Week after week, it would be business as usual, but all of a sudden, one night as I was mopping the floor of the office, which was one of my duties at the station, the police radio scanner went crazy and the code meant that a mean person robbed several businesses all along the Savannah Highway, and he was making his way down Cosgrove Avenue. Sure enough, I had a thought that would come into my head. I had a feeling that he would be over here trying to rob me. I had a lot of cash, and I needed to empty the register, for only a little bit of money, enough just to make change. And so, I began to take out a lot of money out of the register and put a lot of it in the safe.

I noticed a gold looking beat up old car parking alongside the gate. As I had a customer pull up, I had to take care of him, and so I did. And as I got through with him, I noticed that a black man, who wasn't wearing a mask at the time and who seemed harmless enough, asked me for change, and so when I opened the register to give him the change, he pulled out what looked like a brand new, shiny .45-caliber handgun and pointed it at my face. So I did what he told me to do, and when he wanted the money, the best thing that I did was to do just as he said.

My boss said, "I know that you're going through a rough time in your life right now. I can understand that, but I need you. I'm going to make it worth your while to come back to work. Would you please consider it?" I thought for a few minutes and said, "Okay! I know that you can't help it at this time, but I'm going to make sure that you owe me a big one!" The boss paused for a few minutes. Then he said, "All I know, it that I need you and that I would greatly appreciate it if you would come in." I said, "Well, you would have to give me a few minutes to get dressed, and tell these folks my apology, and tell them, that I Have to be off, and go to work." The boss said, "Again, I'm sorry that this happened, but I have no choice in the matter. I hope you and your father understand." As I hung up the phone, I had to admit that I was angry.

My dad was observing me on the phone. He took note of the angry look on my face and asked, "What's the matter son?" I told him, "My sorry boss did something to the temporary person that was hired to take my place for a while." I continued, "I have to report to work right now." My dad, who had a shocked look on his face, said, "You mean to tell me that we have all these people here, and I'm going to have everything to do?" I told him, "I'm afraid that is the way it is, Pop. Someone will just have to be there, because it is a 24/7 type of business." My dad couldn't believe it himself, as he walked away to the living room to give the folks my best regards and tell them that I would have to leave for work."

And as I drove off, he stared at me the whole way to the car. At the time, I was angry. And believe you me, as the car drove out the parking lot and back to the house, I can imagine that he had a hissy fit, and I can imagine what he must've told people after I left, but you know what? I didn't care at the time, because I had a career, waiting for me, and I was glad to put that horror story to rest for a while.

As I entered the door, my mom asked me, "Son, what are you doing home so early?" I told her what happened, and she told me, "Good for you! Now I have raised my baby to be good soul, and he will be right with the Lord. I was glad that happened, because I knew that he would be up to no good." I told my mom, "Well, I'm just glad, that I soon will have another job to fall back on, and that I planned this just right." She agreed with me and told me, "Not to worry. We won't put any pressure on you about the bills, because we know that you don't have any job to go to until you get into boot camp. And please don't forget about me and write to me often." I promised her that I would and went into the bedroom to change into some casual clothes.

In the mailbox, I did receive my last paycheck, and I knew what I had a hankering for, and that would be one of my favorite things. So I got into the car and drove to the nearest BK I could find. I would usually get enough sandwiches to last me several days, and I still say that I have the record for eating the most sandwiches at one restaurant. I would always go to the one on the corner of Orange Grove and Sam Rittneberg. Every now and then, I would enjoy a big Mac attack, but not usually. Since I was rapidly running out of time, I was going to enjoy as many BKs as I could get. No offense to Mom; she could cook and put any restaurant down to size, bit I had an addiction for those things and I didn't know if I would get another one for the next forty-five years.

The boss, later on, came by to see me and asked, "Well, how does it feel to be a hero?" I laughed at him saying, "Quit that. It hurts if I laugh too hard." He chuckled and told me that he was proud of me standing up to the robber as I did, and he said, "When the community finds out hw the robber died, I don't think you have to worry about anybody robbing the station for a long time. He told me that the police were getting on him about not having someone who would be partners with me, so he hired someone to take some of the load off of me. He would assist me in collecting the money, and all I would have to do is pump that gas at night. I told him, "I appreciate it, but like you say, I don't think anybody will mess with me no more, and I needed the money." He didn't like that one bit and urged me to accept his offer, because his mother would insist. I told him, "I don't think my mother knows that after I pay them for staying under their roof that I don't have much money left." After the boss heard I paying to stay in my own home, he didn't much like that. I couldn't help what he did or didn't like. I just knew that it made me a better person to learn to accept my own responsibility. He must've been taught otherwise, and due to the at fact, I can see why his son acts the way he does, and I vowed to myself that I would never act that way.

After two weeks were up, I was visited by the doctor, who had good news for me. He told me, "With all that happened to you, you are considered in my opinion to be of sound mind and body, and you are ready to go home." I was happy to hear that and said, "Yeah!"

When I got back home, my parents made sure I was fed and rested before I returned to work. The doctor wanted me to come by his office to make sure that I was fit to report back to work. After a couple of months of being off, I was getting bored. I felt like a vampire or something ready to pounce on anybody. But at least, I thought, it was good that the boss insisted on me getting some help at night.

Having second thoughts on the matter, I decided that I could disarm the fellow and hold him until the police came. I was thinking that patrolmen were always coming by to shoot the breeze or to buy snacks to help them stay awake. So then I proceeded with my plan. I backhanded him in the face, just enough to stagger him, and I knocked the gun out of his hand. We then proceeded to wrestle along the pavement, while all this was going on a customer pulled up to buy some gas. When he saw the commotion that was going on in the office, he decided to pull out. The reason why I know this because I saw him with the corner of my eye. At least, he didn't help himself to some gas at the same time. Or I guess he got scared that he would be shot or something, while we were struggling. He and I were hitting each other with tremendous blows. I was thinking to myself that I was so glad that my father taught me the art of self defense. When I saw that he left himself wide opened for one last blow, I used the palm of my hand, and with a mighty thrust I hit him with all the force that I could muster right in the nose. He immediately fell backwards a few feet and proceeded to hit his head and could not get up after that. He lay there motionless.

I shook my head and regained my composure, looking down to the floor where he lay. I immediately called the police and told them, "Hey! I am in an emergency here! I have been robbed. I think that the robber is unconscious." The officer on the other line said, "Hang on, sir. I'm going to send an officer to your location. Now, where are you located?" I was totally out of breath, but I said, "I'm at Cosgrove and Windham Drive. And I think that I'm hurt as well. The officer said with concern in his voice, "Just hang on, Mr. Brady. One of the officers knows who you are and told me over the radio, and he told you that he is on the way. And an ambulance will also be on the scene as well." I told him, "Please hurry, because I don't know how long this guy will be knocked out, but I hit him pretty hard with the palm of my hand and I hope he's still here until you get here."

As I entered the courtroom, he was brought in by the police in handcuffs and was told to sit down. As the proceedings were getting underway, the presiding judge entered the courtroom and began to sit down at her bench. The trial didn't last long because after I testified about what happened, he couldn't do anything but tell the judge that happened the way I stated. The judge took no pity on him and said, "Due to the fact that your behavior was that of a child, you will spend some time in jail to think about what you did and to contemplate how you can mend your ways. Not only that, I have decided that you will work out the time that you are in jail to work out all the energy that you seem to have there. Maybe doing some hard work in the hot summer sun will straighten you out and maybe you will be a better person. Also, I feel that you are an angry person and you must have therapy to control that anger.' Then she paused, as she let the defendant tell her whatever he wanted so say. He started to cry and told her, "Please judge, I'm sorry about what I have done, and that it will never happen again." The judge looked at him pretty sternly and told him, "Being sorry, doesn't count around here, especially when you hurt that poor man over there, and you will serve time for what you have done."

After that, I was glad it was over with, but I had to go to work that evening, and this thing had interfered with my sleep. I had not gone to bed yet, and I was about to sleep in the courtroom. The attorney wouldn't let me do that. He would tap me on the shoulder to wake me up and say, "You did a good job in there. Now it's time to give you a lift back to the station, so that you can go home and get some rest." I smiled at him and shook his hand, for bringing me to the courtroom and back and giving me the advice that I needed to gain Mrs. Cannon's favor to put this guy for a while. But the task at hand was to get home, and I couldn't wait.

Just for curiosity, I looked down at the river's marker which told me at the time that the bridge would be safe. As I worked feverishly to get the car hooked up, the policeman was taking his time doing his paper work. As he was delaying me for no telling how long, I decided to look down at the river one more time, and sure enough, the marker moved some, and I decided right then and there to tap on that windshield and ask for the paperwork that I needed so that I could get out of there. I told the officer, "Hey, the bridge is moving, and it is unsafe for both of us to be here. How about give me the paperwork so that I can get out of here?" With the howling wind and the rain, it was hard to carry on a conversation, but I could tell that his face was a lot whiter and the he was having an episode of fear that told him to hurry up. As he wrote down the last bit of information on the report, he told me, "Carry on." I nodded my head in agreement, and with that, I hurried into the wrecker and took off. Again, it was a struggle to come back to the station.

During the next morning and after a rough night, I was exhausted to the point of collapsing. The boss came in, and there was still lingering rain in the air. I just finished pumping gas into a car, when all of a sudden, there was a loud bash that came from the sky, and a transformer pole gave out an illuminating light and the sparks almost made me see my life flash before my eyes.

I was glad to be back to the station. Best of all, I was so glad the storm was over and the night was over. As I told the boss what kind of night that I had, he padded me on the back and told me, "I'm proud of you, and do you have the police report of time that you got the car off the bridge?" I told him, "Yes, I do, and the officer told me to tell you that you can charge anything that would be a fair price." It seemed that a dollar sign flashed in his head, and he was enjoying it.

The police, as they watched, almost felt for me, I would have to walk back to the sidewalk where the wrecker was. The officer said, "I'm sure glad that I'm not you. It must be a tough way to make your living." I told him, "You better believe that, but you know what? I must love my job, just like you guys like your job." The officer laughed and gave me the police report to take back to the station. I would be soaked to the bone and as I pulled out to go back the water would just pour out. As I pulled into the gate, tried to pick a spot where the insurance adjuster with wet clothes on, so I went home to change. As I did so, I noticed that the house had a light on. I thought to myself that it was odd because my parents were on vacation at the time, and I was wondering if the house was broken into. I decided not to park in the drive, but I would park across the street so that no one would expect me to enter the drive. I noticed that the glass was broken, and I was hearing a lot of commotion going on in the house.

I'm glad that the boss installed two-way radio in the wrecker now, because I got in contact with the station. There was a janitor who would be there to do odd jobs for the boss, and as I told him what was going on, he told me that he would call the police to my residence.

The police came with me to the house, and they also heard the noises going on like somebody was tearing the place up. They wanted to kick the door in, so I gave them permission, and as they did they said, "Police, freeze!" And when they said that, the guy froze in place. At the last second, he decided to run, but he was caught.

I always walked over to Dad's room and checked on him to see if he was all right in the morning. As I poked my head into the room, I said, "Good morning, old man, how are you feeling this morning?" He looked over at me, still under the sheets, and said, "Not worth a dern, son." I asked him, "Hey, how would you like some eggs this morning?" He told me, "I think that it would be an excellent idea." I laughed and said, "I guess that means you're not going to turn it down." He told me, "Not on your life." I said, "Okay pop, they will be ready in a few minutes." He nodded his head as if to ay that he understood.

As I prepared him a good meal, and I was able to eat one myself, I started to do the chores in order to get a head start on them, and then I realized that today was the day that I had to get some errands done. I looked as though I was going to have my hands full, but what else is new?

I knew that I still had some time, so I was able to get a lot done, as far as washing clothes, doing the dishes, dusting, and vacuuming. I was already tired and the day wasn't even half over yet. I looked at it this way: paying bills was a good excuse to get out of the house.

It was always great for me to drive my Dodge Dakota sports car, which I had bought recently. I really didn't really enjoy the color; I had to take that awful-looking green color. But there was a bright side to everything. The salesperson at the time told me that red this time of year is like a radar beacon for the police, and green is one of those colors that stay cool during the summer. But I told him, as I could remember, "Green? Don't you have any other color? But I take that back. I don't like white either because it seems that you have to wash it all the time." He agreed with me at the time, but he told me, "No, this is really the only color that I have in this model at this time, but you're getting a brand new car tight off the showroom. This would be something that you would always cherish." I had to admit, I always wondered how they would drive the car out of those showrooms, and now I get to see firsthand how they did it. I can remember being excited as much as I was when I became a father for the first time.

I asked him, "Hey Pop, are you all right? I notice that your skin looks kind of pale there." My dad said, "I'll be okay." As I examined him, I said, "I don't think you're doing so hot, Pop. Maybe, I should call the doctor or something. Right off the bat, he didn't like that idea at all. He continuously told me that he would be all right, so I began to take his word for it and then I proceeded to take my shower and got some fresh clothes. I decided that I would cook him some chicken for dinner, and some rice and beans would probably do the trick. Maybe then he would feel better.

After supper, I noticed that he didn't eat very much, and before I knew it, he started to throw up. At first, I didn't know what to do, but I thought about the little tub, that you bring from the hospital for just that occasion. Sure enough, it worked like a charm. He was finally getting better, and after that episode. I made sure that he received plenty of fluids. I immediately asked him, "Hey Pop, I'm going to get you a glass of water, and I think after that you need to get some rest." He nodded his head in agreement with me, so after I gave him the glass of water, I put him back into the bed.

Later on that night, sometime early in the morning, I would be woken up by a loud bang that sounded like it was in Dad's room. After I went to check on him, I noticed that he had fallen out of the bed. He kept trying to get himself up, and a she did so, I would try to get to him and help him in bed. He wouldn't let me do that, and I said, "Dad, I'm going to call the hospital emergency. I think you need to go there." Again, in a very weak state, he told me in no uncertain terms, "No." The only thing that I could have done was wait until he could have no say at all. That is to say, I would be waiting for him to get unconscious and ten after that, I would be able to call EMS.

In between working on the job and waiting on him when I could, I seemed to have the whole world on my shoulders, but we needed the money. One day, in the hot summer sun, I was ordered to sweep up the pavement or the whole parking lot, because the hot wind during the summer would blow on the asphalt. When that would happen, I had to sweep and clean up the trash. While I was out there, I also had to catch the customers as they pulled into the drive. I can remember it so well, because between the heat and the humidity, it felt like 105 degrees, and I also observed that dust devils would form on the lost next door to us. There I was, by the heat of the day. I stopped to take a breather, and as I looked up, the bright yellow sun would be baking down on me. The reason why is because there were no trees to hide under, so I had no shade to rest under. I also had to shovel the dirt along the edge of the walk way, and I hope that you can imagine that a full garbage can of dirt can be very heavy. That day, I can remember lifting several of those heavy cans. By quitting time, I could only get to the first driveway, but no matter, I was thinking to myself that it looked pretty good. And if you remember those old mom-and-pop gas stations, there would be grassy area in front or next to the highway. I also had to make sure that the excess grass growing along the side of the curb had to be cleared of all grass and that the dirt had to be swept off and dumped in the dumpster. But that would have to wait for another day.

I couldn't wait to get home to Pop. I knew that I left him plenty of drink and snacks, so that he could get by until I came home and cook him supper. I was thinking to myself as I would be driving home and saying things like, "Just hang on, Dad. I'll be right home in a few minutes, just hang on."

Sure enough, when I popped my head in the door, my dad said, "Son is that you? You were right boy, you had enough food and drinks to last me, and I thank you!" I finally, entered his room and said, "Hey Pop, how are you feeling today?" My dad looked up at me and I could tell that he was really weak, but I noticed that he had plenty to eat.

Later on during the week, a lady pulled in the drive and wanted to fill up. At the time, I noticed that she had her windshield still up and that she looked drunk or stoned, and that I figured that I would have a hard time with her. After I did everything, I told her the price of the gas, and she just looked at me funny and drove on without paying for her gas, and she just looked at me funny and drove on without paying for her gas. It kind of took me by surprise, but my initial reaction was to pull out my gun. When

I did, I hesitated for a split second, and when she was about to pull out of the drive, I shot at the back tire. And saying a few favorable words, I shot the other back tire. I disabled her car from going anywhere, and I ran into the office to call the police. When the police came, they were at the car in a few minutes with the lights flashing. They looked throughout her car, and wouldn't you know it? She had taken off, but they found she had drugs in her possession. My boss was so pleased, because I was the one that they wanted to tow the car. And that it would be on her, if they ever caught her that is.

All of sudden, the police department had a newfound respect for me. They would come by the station at night and shoot the breeze and hang around the station at certain times of the night, and it would make the night go a little bit faster for me and them.

On a Saturday night, the boss told me that they were expecting a call that night, and that they would have some of the day shift employees to handle some of the tow jobs from this particular club on the old Navy base. Sure enough later on that night, the call came in, and several cars had to be towed from the lot because they were parked there without the owner of the property's permission. As they started coming in with the cars, I opened the gate to let them in, and he told me, "Now Scott, I'm trusting you to collect the tow from these people when they come in tonight for their cars. I'm here to warn you that they might be rough on you, and I'm hoping that you can handle it."

I thought a lot of Debbie, but I learned a shocker. She was dating my boss, and I wondered about that. Because I thought the boss was married. I always heard my boss's last name and never really paid attention to his first name. As I went home from work that day, I noticed that when the person who gave me the interview had provided me with a paper with the boss's name on it. I decided to play detective work, and look at it to see if it had a first name on it like I thought. And sure enough, it did. "What do you know?" I said to myself. He did have a first name. I'm wondering if both men's first names were the same. I decided that it was none of my business; he was the one that would have to live with his conscience and that he would be the one to answer to the Lord. But it seemed strange to me, and I wondered if the boss's wife had any suspicion of what was going on. And something funny came to my mind, if the boss listened to my dad and told him that I should work at night to forget about my mom's death, then maybe, it should be the boss who needed to work all day night and day in order for him not to get in trouble for running around on his wife. The thing is I had to snicker to myself, contemplating the domestic squabble that would be in his future.

Well, during the week, I didn't know if I could survive working all-nighters during the week, as well as my regular shift, but I was glad that things were coming back to normal. All the distant relatives were gone back to wherever they came from, and Dad and I would have more time together to make up for anything that we may have said to one another. I thought that it was high time for us to spend some time together, and to find out how things were between us.

I still had my boat, and I figured that fishing would be the thing that would bring us closer. It was summer again, and being out in the middle of the ocean would be the best medicine I could think of. So I grabbed Dad one morning from getting off work and said, "Hey, old man, how about we get the boat all shipped up and shaped up for the water and the two of us to deep sea fishing?"

As I pulled in the drive at work, I noticed that the boss was waiting for me. As I entered the office, he told me, "Your father didn't want me to tell you this, but before you judge me and have ill feelings toward me, I just wanted to tell you that it was your father who called me a while back and told me to keep you busy. He thought that by working it would keep your mind off things that were going on, and what it would ease your grieving period." As you can tell right now, I was angry at him and myself. I said "How dare he do things behind my back? I needed to grieve over Mother just like he does. I loved her just liked he did, but I could understand that they were man and wife for years. But he should let me deal with the situation in my own way. I am a grown man now, and not a child." The more I thought about it, the angrier I became. But after a while, I had to realize that he was my father, and hat maybe I was too hasty in judgment.

During the longest and most difficult night that I ever experienced, somebody walking in the dark came up to the office, and it turned out to be a friend of mine, who knew what I was going through with my boss. She sat down with me and we began talking.

Her name was Debbie. She was a very nice, shapely blonde who cared about me a lot, and like I said before, who was a regular customer and knew my boss. She would tell me in a peppy voice that would wake me up, "Well hello there, stranger. I haven't seen you in a couple of nights. What's going on?" I explained, "Well how about this for a start? I don't know if you know this or not, but my mom passed on, and she was just buried today. And also, I was called into work, because I guess that I'm always going to have the title of being the black sheep of the family." Debbie's jaw dropped like a rock and said, "You mean to tell me that Sam wouldn't let you have the night off?" I told her, "No, it gets better than that. I just want to let you know that my dad didn't want me around with the family, so he suggested to my boss that I should work through this difficult time to get over my mom's death."

May I add that Debbie's face had a pale expression as she tried to think of something to cheer me up and that could somehow get me to forgive my dad for what he did. She told me, "Well, you know Scott, it was probably that your dad thought working would keep you busy and take your mind off things." Looking at her, I said, "I appreciate what you are telling me, but I can't help but wonder whether or not Dad really wanted me or if he wished that I were dead." Debbie, with disbelief on her face, said, "I can't believe that you would say anything like that about your dad. I'm pretty sure that he would only have your best interest at heart, because he thought that you would get over your mom's death quicker." I looked at her with one of those doubtful looks, as she continued, "You may not believe me, Scott Brady, but I think that you should appreciate your dad even more, and I'll say it again. I think that he loves you very much, and I do think that he thinks that you would get over this difficult time quicker this way." I told her, "Well, I don't think that being here is going to ever make me forget my mom. In fact, I don't think I will ever forget her, because I still think that she cared for me more than Dad."

Debbie couldn't believe how stubborn I could be. I couldn't help it because as I understand it, I have Irish Scottish ancestry, and I would always have that instinct to be stubborn and to fly off the handle and to fight. But I can say that Debbie had patience with me, and tried to console me as much as possible, especially during this time of my life. She would come to the station almost every night that I worked and talk to me one on one, and I think to this day that it helped me a lot.

Everyone, while I was making the announcement, had those shocked looks on their faces. I told them that it wasn't my boss's fault. "This happens, but someone has to be there, and I guess that I'm elected to the post. I do apologize that I won't be with all of you, but in case you're gone when I come back in the morning. I just want everyone to know that my father and I do appreciate you coming and giving us your support. And to those of you who are staying awhile with us, I just want to let you know that I'm going to be back tomorrow morning somewhere around 7:00 a.m. in the morning." I continued, "So I shall see you then, but when you are up, I'm going to be in the bed. I want to end this by saying good night."

I hurriedly left the room to change into my work uniform. As I left, I could hear them talking and saying things like "The nerve of his boss to make him work on the eve of his mother's death." But the men's side would say, "Well, maybe this will be a way to occupy his mind and keep him busy enough that his grief period will be a brief one." Then again, the female side would say, "May I remind you that we are talking about his mother, and that's someone who you should be one for on a time like this." Then the male side would come back with, "Well, someone's got to do the job, and it just as well may be him, he's still making money." Then the female of the crowd would come back at their husband's and say, "It's his mother for God's sake. Can't you get that through your head? And he needs to be here for his father." As they continued, "He's the one that's hurting too, and he could use his help right now." And of course in these kinds of get-togethers, you're going to have a lot of that kind of drama going around. But it seems that it was my decision, and by the way, jobs in any time period I have noticed are very hard to come by. So what is a person to do in this situation? But as you would read on, there would be a twist that you're not going to be prepared for.

After getting home from work that afternoon, my dad warned me that we had a little get-together with Lydia on a Friday night, and the he would appreciate it if I would come. I was dressed and ready to go. But all the while, I kept having the feeling that someone was watching me. I turned around, and lo and behold, it was my dad kind of giving me the eye. I told him, "And what are you supposed to be looking at?" He was looking at something of me. Then, he finally spoke, "Well son, I'm just checking and making sure that you're not going to be embarrassing me in front of Lydia and her daughter this evening." I stared Dad down and I told him, "Look Dad, I'm a grown man, and I do think that after four years in the military, and a lot of time of maturity, should tell you that I'm not going to be the one spoiling your evening." I continued, "As a matter of fact, I did take a bath. I also shaved pretty good, and I also would like to let you know that I'm wearing a dress shirt and dress slacks, so I don't know what else to do. Maybe it will be too fancy for me, and I shouldn't go. You make me feel as though I'm being inspected by a general or something." My dad said, "Oh son, behave yourself. I just want to make sure everything goes according to plan." I had my turn to look at him funny, and I said, "Well, Dad, don't worry, especially about me. I will act charming, and I won't embarrass you too bad either." My dad said, "Well thank you for that anyway son, because I think a lot of her, and I want you to like her a lot too, and maybe even love her." I told dad, "We would have to wait to see on that Dad. It takes time and a lot of effort on both of us to see if this works."

As we entered the door, Lydia said, "Well, look at both of you. Both of you look so nice." Both of us smiled and said, "Thank you." My dad said, "Something smells so wonderful in the kitchen, now don't it, son?" I looked at Dad like he was putting me on the spot and said, "Oh yeah, Pop, it sure does. What's cooking, good-looking?" Lydia laughed and said, "It's a rump roast in the oven with all the fixings." I told her, "I love rump roast, ma'am."

Sure enough, later on that night, the cars started to come in. people were lining up to pay their tow bill, and a lot of them, according to my survey, weren't too pleased about paying their bill. The reason that I'm saying that is because you feel the same way, I guess, when you pay any bill. It seems like anytime you have to stand in line, for any length of time to pay any bill, it brings out the worst in you. In one instance, one person wasn't very happy about the situation and tried to drive off with his car. Apparently, he had a second set of keys with him. I immediately ran to get behind his car and stopped him from driving off by pulling my gun out and telling him to halt. When he didn't do that, he started to come out of the car, and when he did, I made the mistake of putting my gun in the holster. He then proceeded to hit me constantly, but he really didn't have much of a punch. I was really in good shape and was able to withstand any kind of punch that he could throw. After wearing himself out, he started to walk to the car that brought him to the station, and they started to drive off. I wrote down the owner's license plate number, and I then called the police.

The police came within a few minutes and took out the report about what happened. Then they took off, but within a few minutes I received the call that he was arrested and was not able to get out on bond.

A few days later, I was scheduled to report in for court that morning to testify, and to tell my side of the story about what happened. Our esteemed judge at the time was Judge Cannon, who had a reputation of being tough and wouldn't take any guff from anyone, or you would go straightaway to jail.

After the attorney brought me back, the boss asked me, "Well, how did things go in there? Did that guy pay for what he did to you?" I told him, "Hey boss, I think that with all the risks that I'm taking each night on this job, I deserve a raise."

My boss looked at me like they were fighting words. But I meant what I said. I was not backing down on my decision. The boss didn't know what went on there, night after night, and also the kind of characters that came into the station was unreal. The boss also said, "I know that you are risking you're life for a little pay, but I can't afford to give you anything right now. It's just impossible for me to give you the raise that you want." After he said that, I was getting frustrated to say the least, but I gritted my teeth and walked off. The boss shook his head, turned the other way, and walked off.

After getting up at the usual time in the night to get ready for work, I watched an AD that appeared on TV screen, and it gave me a good idea. The AD was about joining the military and seeing the world. More specifically, it was an AD about the Navy. I grew up as a Navy brat with my dad being in security and with his time in the service. I wanted to follow in his footsteps. I decided that I would give them a call and find out more about this.

As I was getting out of the car, I can feel the heavy gushes of the wind that blew across the parking lot. I told one of the people who was getting off from the afternoon shift, "Wow, this is a wild and wooly storm, and it is going to be wicked before this night is through." The worker laughed and told me, "Hey, it is rough for everybody, but it looks like you are going to have the roughest night. I wish you good luck, because the wind speed will be 95mph." I was having to give him one of those disgusting looks that told him, "Oh Lord, why me?

As the night went on, we stayed opened to pump gas as long as the power would stay on. And as usual, I was soaked to the bone at this time. I could feel and taste the stinging rain as it blew hard against my face. But when the midnight hour rolled around, the power blew out, and I immediately started the station on shutdown mode. By now it was pouring rain, and also it was thundering and lightning badly. As I was sitting and monitoring the weather, the crew from Good Morning America came bursting into the station, wearing heavy duty raincoats, as if they had experience doing these storms. I noticed one of them, for he was a star on one of those TV shows for a long time, and I told him how much I loved his show and I was a fan of his. He thanked me and asked me how I could work in this kind of weather. I told him, "I have a duty to do, and I saw that somebody had to be out here, so I guess it had to be me." And at that point, a strong gust of wind came and blew opened the front door of the place, and then there was a huge gush of water blowing in. And when the water blew in, it went under the coffee machine and blew up. And when it made this horrific noise, little BooBoo ran as hard as she could into the back room of the garage, and from then on it was silent. The guys from the TV show said that it was time to get some pictures of the storm and that I should watch it on TV.

Going back to work on the next day with all of this hanging over me, I felt like standing up somewhere and screaming out, "Why me!" But I knew that it wouldn't go any good, and that I had to be strong for both of us. All I knew was to do the task at hand and that was to finish sweeping the driveway. During the time that I was doing this, I noticed something after I picked up a heavy can of dirt. All of a sudden, I felt like I was going to pass out. I stood there trying to regain my strength, I decided that I would take a few steps, but when I did, I fell right on the ground. The boss noticed what happened, came to me, helped me up, and said, "Are you all right?" I told him, "Not really. All of a sudden, I felt kind of weak, like I was going to pass out." The boss told me, "I think that the sun may be getting to you. After all, this job isn't easy, especially out her today." I agreed with him, and he suggested that since it was lunch time that I should go sit in the air conditioner and cool off. He also told me, "We are also deciding what we are going to have for lunch." And after standing and talking with him, I said, "I sure could go for a hamburger right now." The boss laughed and said, "Well, maybe we can get that arranged for you."

After eating a hot lunch, I felt better for a long time. In fact, I was feeling great. And by the time I got off, I noticed the date on my watch, and I thought to myself, in a cheerful sort of way, that today was Friday, and the weekend was finally here. Better yet, it was payday as well. But all of a sudden, reality set in. With me being busy with Dad, the bills were not paid, and I was glad to have the day off to pay those bills.

Finally, getting off time arrived, and I was so glad to get home and take a shower and check on Dad to see if he would be all right. Sure enough, as I entered his room he was still in the bed resting. I decided that I would not wake him. But I was glad that he made it through his ordeal, and that he was able to get a ride home. I'm so glad that we were blessed with real good neighbors.

Every night, I would check out the tow yard. And every night, it would be the same: boring. I kept wondering how long it would be before something happened. Sure enough, one night when I was checking the lot, I noticed movement in one of the cars, kind of way down in the lot. I couldn't make out exactly what it was, so I decided, that the best thing would be for me to close the station temporarily and check it out. As I pumped the gas for a few of the cars that would show up I took the time to shut down the station. I had second thoughts about whether or not I should do that, soothe boss told me on the phone, "Scott, you must check the yard one more time, and if you see any movement in the car, you must go down and check it up close before you call the police." Sure enough, I walked back to the fence, and I noticed again a lot of movement in the car. As I walked back to the station, I started to close it down for a few minutes, so I can go ahead and check it out.

As I walked down to the car and got a closer look, I noticed the car had a bundle in the back seat. After some more movement in the car, I noticed that it was a man, who looked like one of the hobos of the town.

I immediately ran back to the office and called the police to come and get him. This time the police didn't respond as fast as usual, and I kept checking the car and sure enough he was still in the car, and I guess that the car was too small for his big frame and that he was trying to get comfortable and could not.

Finally, the police showed and arrested him for trespassing. Again I had to appear in court and tell the court what happened, so they could lock him up. Again the lawyer was kind enough to take me to court and back to the office. The lawyer said, "This seems like déjà vu. How have you been, young man?" I told him that I was fine, and I was eager to get started with this so that I could get back in bed. He told me, "Well, I can't blame you for that, son. I guarantee you that this will be only a formality." I told him that I hope that you are right, and we both laughed about it.

That night, as I arrived to go to work, I noticed something weird in the tow yard. After everyone left, I decided to investigate. As BooBoo and I stopped at the fence, with the yard all lit up, I could not believe my eyes. Underneath a car was a pair of sneakers with their toes pointing straight up in the air as if he was telling me that he wasn't worried about getting caught. I sneaked back into the office and told the police that I spotted someone in the yard, trying to steal parts out of the car. Pretty soon, the police arrived into the drive and as I instructed to the dispatcher, they came not running their lights or sirens because I told them maybe it would scare him off.

I instructed the police to follow me down into the yard. Sure enough, there he was, still under the car trying to get a part, but probably without any experience under his belt. It was taking him a long time to get the part that he was after. He was totally unaware that he was surrounded by not only the police but I was down there as well. One of the police officers tapped him on the foot with his shoe and told him, "Hey, you! How about getting from underneath the car? This is the police ordering you from under the car now." As he was trying to pull himself out from underneath the car, the police officer helped him along by grabbing his leg and started pulling him out with one good pull. You should have seen the scared look that he had on his face. I told the police, "A gang of boys has been stealing from this yard for a while, and I think that if you question him you will find out that there is more than one." The police thanked me, and I told them that I had to go back to the station and open it back up for business.

One of the police officers commented that I was pretty brave to be working at his job at night in this neighborhood. I told him, "Well, I wish that you all would tell my boss this because he will not give me a raise, and I should be able to get one." The police were all in agreement, and they also told me that they would back me up. So, when the next morning came, a line of police cars lined up at the station, and the boss, looking out the window, had a scared look about him as if he was going to be arrested. Naturally, I was going home at this time, and I didn't know that this was going to happen. After a long conversation with the police department, my boss decided that it was time for me to get a raise. And when he made that decision, I think it delayed me from doing what I intended to do that day, and the Navy career would have to wait.

The next few nights were quite. Everything was normal finally, but I was wondering for how long. Sure enough, a long white limousine pulled into the drive and wanted a fill up. A black person got out of the back seat, and I had a suspicion that he was a pimp. Sure enough, he opened the door on the other side and out came a beautiful black girl. They were wearing the typical getup of the day. You know the 70s look. The woman even had a fur coat on, and during these times, everything was inflated to the point to where it was rough enough just surviving for the most common fold. But I didn't think much about it because he seemed to be a nice guy as far as I was concerned. And sure enough, I was a good judge of people, because after I told him the price of the gas, he gave me a hundred dollar bill and told me to keep the change. He must have been happy with the service because he kept coming back almost every night.

I told him that I believed that this was done by the creeps where I towed the car from the Kangaroo Club. The boss agreed with me and started to call the police so that he could make a complete report and so that he could get everything covered by insurance. When the police came, they asked me if I could give a description of the vehicle, but the only thing I could tell was that I was face first on the ground and wasn't able to tell them anything. But I believed that the people that were towed or about to be towed from the Kangaroo Club would be the ones I would go after. After hearing me and what I had to say, they told my boss, "Without any description we have nothing to go on." But they would be glad to make out the report for insurance purposes. I told the boss that I was sorry and that I had a feeling that it would happen because those guys were flaky. The boss that it would happen because those guys were flaky. The boss agreed with me and told me to go home and get some rest.

When I got back home, I felt like I should quit this job or ask for more money than what I was getting. In my time, the minimum wage would pay little more than three dollars per hour. But the fringe benefits were not bad. I did also get to play with the puppy and take care of her as well. All I knew is that I had a lot to tell my mom and pop after I got home.

I entered the kitchen door and waked up finally to the fact that I was home finally and that I had a good breakfast waiting for me. My mom gave me a big hug and asked me how my day went and I told her that I was shot at last night. She was shook up a little bit and asked me if I was all right. I told her that I was, but the job would prove to be dangerous for the little money that I would be getting. She asked me if I wanted to quit, and I told her no. But that I had a feeling that this job would give me a lot of interesting stories to tell, and my instincts a lot of the time were right.

I unhooked the car and got back into the vehicle and drove away. I rushed back to see if anyone broke into the yard where all the cares were. I didn't like the responsibility of towing cars because it took me away from guarding the cars waiting to be collected. And a lot of the insurance companies took their time into giving him the money for getting all the calls, which made him to get up all hours of the night. As I pulled into the drive, I noticed that everything so far was A. okay! I went back into the office and made a full report of the job I had to do.

I finished up the report, and then I started to spend a lot of time getting to know BooBoo, who was a chocolate Lab. He, the boss, got her when she was a puppy. She took a liking to me right off. We played for a little bit while there was nothing going on. I noticed in the corner of my eye a muzzle flash, I knew instantly that it was a gun, but it was weird because at first I didn't hear a sound. I didn't hear anything until they were heading to the door. I immediately ducked and got flat on my stomach and prayed that they would not shoot me. I almost didn't duck in time because after they left I noticed that one of the bullet holes was aimed right at my head. I was so lucky, or was blessed by the Lord. All I knew was I just couldn't wait for the next morning so I could go home. I had my life flash before my eyes, and I would cheat death this time. Poor BooBoo was so scared that she ran into the jeep that was in the garage, where it was safe. As far as BooBoo was concerned, it was the best place to be.

By the time the next morning came around, the boss pulled into the drive as usual around 7:00 a.m., and he had a shocked look about him as he limped along. He looked around at all the damage and said, "My God, you weren't kidding. Are you all right? Oh my God, you were almost shot in the head. That bullet hole is at the door entrance."

When I pulled into the drive, I saw several police cars on the scene. As I got out of the vehicle, one of the policemen asked me to stand by and wait a few minutes. As I waited, I noticed that they were waiting too. I decided to walk over and talk to them and see what was going on. I asked them, "What are you guys doing?" They told me that they were going to let me tow the car, but the owners of the auto would not come out, so they told the owner of the club that the vehicle in question would be towed off, if the owners did not come out of the club in a few minutes. As I waited, they finally gave me the signal to go ahead and hook it up. They started to cuss me out with flavorful words, which I just ignored. As they went on and on, the police told me to come where the action was. I told them I had to call my boss on the radio. The police noted that I could charge any price that I wanted.

When I contacted my boss, he told me that the price was one hundred and fifty dollars and that I was to be the one to collect it. As I walked back to where the action was, the police asked, "Well, Mr. Brady, what is your price?" I looked at the guys that I would have to deal with and said, "Well, the boss told me that the charge would be one hundred and fifty dollars, and it will be payable in cash."

After I said that, I was told a few metaphors of which I will leave to your imagination, but after a while, it was agreed and all of the parties involved started to pull out the cash that they all had together. After all that, they managed to come up with the loot. And after I collected the money, I wrote them a receipt to say that they did pay, and I told them, "You can probably get with your insurance company and see if you can't get your money back." I could tell that they were none too happy about the situation, and that I was glad that the bill would be paid here instead of the office, where I could have been killed.

As we were sitting, the police brought out the man who was trying to sleep in the car. They took off his handcuffs and told him to sit down and be quiet and to only talk when the judge asked him something. The man did what he was told to do. As he was settling in his chair, the judge entered the courtroom, and the judge's name was—you are right. You all are getting pretty good at this. Her name was Judge Cannon, and as she came into the courtroom, we were told to rise. When she sat down at the bench, she asked what the next case was. The officer instructed her that it would be our case that would be next on the docket. She asked if all the parties were present, and the officer told her that they were. She told me to come to the stand, and as I did so, she said, "You are beginning to be a regular around here, aren't you?" I told her, "Yes ma'am, but you know I always loved to come to our courtroom and see the Mona Lisa work." She said, "Flattery will get you everywhere, Mr. Brady." She went on. "Now tell us in your words, sir, what went on on the night in question." I said, "Well your honor, it's like this. I noticed the defendant moving quite a bit in the car, and that is what caught him, I guess. He didn't mean any harm, but he was trespassing on our property." She looked at the defendant and said, "Don't you know that it's dangerous to sleep in those cars? You don't know what might be in those things. There could be a snake or anything in them. Therefore, you will not have to work or worry about spending the next thirty days behind bars. That way, I know you'll have a place to stay." After that was done, I was again glad to come home to a meal and go to bed. I always wonder what the next night would bring.

During the winter months, I always seem to have fun on the job. You see there is an area down the road from the station, and this area is called the "duck pond." The reason why it's called this is because all year long, every Saturday night, the drunks seemed to want to make a right turn at this area, and when they did this, they would end up in the middle of the duck pond. It was fun because I would have to drag out the chains and go into the pond, and it would be thirty degrees at night and you would get soaked trying to get the chains where the chassis was or under the back bumper. You almost had to be a deep sea diver to get the chains hooked up to the car.

After gaining some experience on the job, the boss was confident that I could handle pumping gas and towing cars all in the same night. I was extremely nervous about handling so much responsibility, and I wanted a raise if he wanted me to start doing this. He told me that he had faith in my ability and that if would not be that bad, "For you see it will be late at night and I don't think that it will be that busy." I tried to believe that knew what he was talking about, but somehow I didn't think that he did. He also told me that he wanted me to carry a gun for protection on the job. That didn't make me feel any better. I didn't like thinking I could hurt or kill somebody because I was raised on the farm and I was taught how to use firearms. The boss also told me, "With my influence I would be able to let you carry a gun on my property, and if you had to use it, you would not be in trouble at all." I told the boss, "I hope you are right about this because I sure don't wasn't to kill anybody." He smiled and patted me on the shoulder and reassured me that I wouldn't get in any trouble and that he had confidence that I would use common horse sense about it.

Well, here I am with a gun at my side. I had to get used to this .38 Smith & Wesson because I lost some weight, and it was pulling my pants down to the point that instead of getting in trouble over using a gun, the gun might get me in trouble for indecent exposure. The place was lighted up and opened for the first time for an all-nighter. People could finally buy gas here all night if they wanted to, and to get full treatment to boot. That is to say they would be bale to get their oil checked and everything else, like they could do in the day time.

During the night, it seemed to go smoothly. When all of a sudden a car finally pulled into the station at 2:00 a.m., and wouldn't you know it? On a Friday night, the first car that pulled up would be full of strippers. I was a single man too. I couldn't believe it. They told me to fill it up, and I was a little shaky, of course, because you see they were almost naked in the car, but I didn't refuse their business. I filled it up, checked their tires, and checked their oil for them. And after I washed the windshield, I went to take the hose out of the car, and told her the charge was $32.50. She looked at the bill, and it was a 50-dollar bill. I almost fainted. She didn't have to tip me because it was a pleasure to be surrounded by such beauty. After she pulled out of the drive, I went to the office and took out the change and put it into my pocket because I figured if she wanted to do this, I wasn't going to look a gift horse in the mouth.

After a few minutes of waiting, I found myself feeling very weak, and then I found myself falling to the floor. As you can tell, I didn't know it at the time, but when I knocked the gun out of his hand, the gun went off. I found myself bleeding in the left side of my body. As I collapsed on the floor, here came the cavalry. Two police cars and on EMS vehicle came to our aid. As

they entered the building, they were shocked to find me
lying on the floor with a lot of blood loss to boot. The
policeman, Chuck, who knew me by hanging around the
station at night, said, "Oh my God, I can't believe the
mess in here!" He noticed me on the floor with a lot of
blood on me and said, "You guys come in here and give
assistance right away." The EMS workers ran into the
office, looking around at the situation they were getting
into. One of the EMS workers came towards me and
noticed that he needed to stabilize me and needed to get
me to the hospital right away. His partner looked at the
robber and said "Oh my god, this man is dead over here!"
The other EMS as I get this man ready for transport, I'll
check him out too." The partner told him, "Well, partner,
I know dead when I see dead, and this guy is dead." The
other EMS worker, who got me ready to go, walked over
to his partner and said, "Hey! You are right. He is dead
as a doornail all right, and he's not even shot. He must
have been killed by the other guy with his bare hands.
Remind me not to get Scott angry with me. Okay?" The
partner laughed as they told Chuck that he needed to
get a coroner out there because he had a corpse in there.
Chuck said, "You're kidding, what happened?" The EMS
worker told Chuck that, "Apparently during the fight,
your friend over there killed the robber with his bare
hands." Chuck goes, "WOW!"

Chuck went immediately to his cruiser and asked
that the coroner and the homicide squad be called to the
scene. As they arrived, the officer showed them where
the crime scene was, and as they roped off the area to
collect evidence and heard how the robber was killed, the

officers shook their heads and were thinking the same as the EMS workers were.

The boss received the call at 4 in the morning, and when he answered the phone and said "Hello," the officer told him what happened. On the other line the boss stated, "What? Is Scott all right?" The officer told him that I was at MUSC hospital and judgment of the case was that I was considered shot and in stable condition.

As I arrived at the hospital, emergency staff immediately continued to work on me and prepare me for surgery, as they were getting ready to get the bullet out. The doctor and staff found out the information about what happened during the robbery and were shocked and proud of working on someone who had developed a reputation of being in a hero status. The doctor told the nurses to really see to my needs and to make sure that my parents were notified. They were ready to roll me into the operating room and proceeded to take out the bullet in my side, "Oh my God!" And as he got out of the wrecker, he walked over to where the police were and was getting the gist about what happened that evening. He told them that I was getting treated as we spoke. My Dad, who received the word, woke up Mother, and they both immediately got up and were getting ready to go to the hospital. My dad who saw the police at the station told my mother, "I'm going to find out what the hell happened here." My mother was quiet and shocked. She said, "Cecil, I want to go to the hospital, I don't care about the other. You should let the police handle it. I want to see my son, and I want to make sure he is all right and I want to be with him!" After drilling her point home to my dad, He finally decided that it would be the right thing to do. My mom agreed to that, so they went on to the hospital.

As they entered the hospital, they immediately went to the nurse who was standing at the counter writing a report about something, looked up and said, "May I help you please?" My mother, who was getting teary eyed by now, excitedly said, "I want to see my son." The nurse said, "And what would be your son's name?" My mother said, "His name is Scott Brady, and he was injured during a robbery at the gas station where he worked tonight." The nurse said, "Oh, he is still in surgery, and the doctor will fill you in as soon as he can." My mother and father both breathed a sigh of relief and asked if they could sit down somewhere and wait for the doctor. She showed them an area where they could sit, and they did so and started the long wait.

After a period of time, the doctor, who got the word that my parent's were there, strolled out in a hurry to where they were sitting and said, "Mr. and Mrs. Brady, your son is fine. He had a bullet in his left rib area. He has to stay in the hospital for a while, a week or so, until he can come home." My parents asked if they could see me, and the doctor agreed. But he stipulated that I would be out still and that it would be in the morning before I would be able to make sense of anything.

The doctor also told them that would be better to come see me in the morning after they checked in on me that night. My mother, who was getting over the idea that I was in grave danger and relaxed to the point of being confident that I would be all right, agreed with the doctor and proceeded to my room, where I was still out like a light. At this time I was having a dream where I was walking that stairway to heaven, and when I went up to the pearly gates, they opened and I was ready to come on in. But when I got there, the big man himself stood in from of me and told me that I wasn't ready to come to this plane yet. So I turned around and started to walk to my body. And as that happened, I started to wake up, and the nurse who was standing by me said, "Now be calm Mr. Brady, you are all right, and you young man need to go back to sleep and get your rest." I muttered groggily, "My parents, my parents." The nurse said, "Your parents were just here, and they know you are trying to recuperate and that you're just fine. So go back to sleep." As I dozed back off to sleep, I couldn't wait to get back home, but who was to think I would have a night like this?

As I woke up the next morning, I found out what happened. While watching the morning updates on the tub, I found out the robber was caught and the station person was injured. The door opened, and Chuck, the police officer I knew, came in an asked me if I was all right. I told him I had had better in and asked me if I was all right. I told him I had had better days. He told me about what happened and wanted to ask me if he was right. I tile him that the guy tried to rob me last night when I was on duty, and I thought I could subdue him if they caught him.

Chuck not only told me that they caught him, but I killed him with my bare hands. I was shocked to hear what I did and was worried about me getting into any trouble. He assured me that the detectives working on the case had figured out that it was self defense, and that the coroner said that a blow to the nose which broke that cartilage was the cause of the hemorrhage which caused him to die.

There was no question, in their opinion, that it was self-defense and that I should be all right, and that the mayor of the town wanted to give me a citation for bravery. I told him, "I don't think that killing someone constituted a citation of merit." Chuck disagreed. He told me, "If you hadn't stopped this individual, there is no telling what he could have done before the night was over. The police appreciate what you did in risking your life, but next time, how about just give him the money. You only had twenty dollars and some change to begin with."

I was so glad to get that awful experience out of my life. I thought at the time I didn't have anything to lose by jumping him, because I thought for sure he would kill me in a heartbeat. He didn't even attempt to wear something over his head; maybe he thought that he didn't have anything to lose because he was so bold in his way of robbing all the places. Maybe, in my opinion, he wanted someone to catch him. I'm just sorry that it came to me killing him with my bare hands. You see my dad served in the military during WWII, and he would tell me all kinds of stories about the war. He was also a judo expert and instructor. During my childhood he taught me the fine art of self-defense and also boxing. I can remember that every night before he when to bed he would do one hundred push ups, and because I admired him and looked up to him, I joined in and we both did the same amount of pushups together.

Being as young as I was, I thought I could do as many push-ups as my dad, but I found out that I couldn't at first.

I would be sore. I can remember my mother would have to rub solstice on my body and tell me that I was not dad. Maybe when I got a little bit older, I would be able to do a hundred pushups. But after a time, my muscles got used to it, and before long my body would finally get adjusted to it. After a period of time, my dad finally quit doing them because of an experience he had breaking up a fight at the CO club at the old Navy base. A young sailor tried to attack him and resisted arrest, and when he took his bare hands and hit the sailor, he almost ended his life. He has always urged me to quit working out, but to this day I enjoy working out and I will continue to do it. He's not happy right now, but it is my life and I feel that it will not hurt me in the long run to continue to work out.

As I entered the door, I noticed that there was someone already sitting at the chair next to the garage where the cars were being worked on. I said, "Can I help you?" He looked at me while he was petting the dog, and he said, "Hey, I'm the new help that is supposed to give you a hand." I told him, "Yeah, I guess he's nervous, especially with me getting robbed and all." He nodded his head in agreement and noticed the gun that was on my side. I guess he started to get a little nervous about me with a handgun and said, "Why are you carrying a gun? Don't you know those things are dangerous?" I told him, "No not really. I've been around guns all my life, and I know what I'm doing with them. Besides the boss told me to wear this thing to warn off robbers and the like. You should be worried about getting into a battle with me because the last guy that had a fight with me was killed, kinda in the area where you are standing now."

As the night went along, we were getting to know one another, and we were telling each other stories about the previous jobs that we had. I noticed that he had a pizza delivery job where the pay was good, but he was getting into neighborhoods that were like war zones. I had an idea that I would pass onto the boss. My idea was to open the garage at night and to close it when it was so late that we would not get any parts stolen.

The boss agreed with me and said that my duties would be the same, but my partner who used to be a mechanic and knew how to do simple things on the auto such as tires, wipers, and change oil, would do those things. I would collect on the bills and pump. And for thinking of the idea, if it panned out for the first month, he would make sure that I would get a raise. I was smiling ear to ear when I heard those words, and I made a list of the things that I could do with the money. I also wanted bring up the idea with my mom and dad that I wanted a dog. I wanted one of those Doberman pinchers, but I knew that I may have a fight for one when I got home in the morning. I was tired of being told what to do. The Navy career was looking better and better now.

I thanked him for coming by, and they told me because I was so nice that they would mention me on TV and that they would also plug the station's name. All of a sudden, I was surprised that the phone rang. I picked up the receiver and answered, "Hello. Can I help you?" The person on the other end was with the Charleston County Sheriff's department, and they needed a tow truck to pick u a car at the Cooper River Bridge. I told them, "Hey, there is a bad storm going, and you expect me to pick up somebody who should have never been out there in the first place." The officer told me, "I know that it is a rough night, but we need that part of the road cleared up in the morning or the flow of traffic will be interrupted." I told him, "I will do it to help you guys out, but I'm risking life and limb to help you out." The officer acted grateful after he had to do his sale pitch, and he told me "We appreciate it, and you can tell the boss he can charge any fair price that he wishes." I told him that I appreciated it, and as I hung up, I said, "Of all the times someone had to go sightseeing, it would have to be tonight." I hoped that they were in jail for a long time.

I had a battle on my hands. I had to go down into the towing yard to pick up the wrecker, but first had to open the gate in the driving rain, back the wrecker up, close the gate and finally start on my way to get the sightseer.

As I was driving down, the rain washed out several roads to the point of being impassible. It was frustrating to even get on the road to the Old Cooper River Bridge, but in all the pouring water, I could only see the flashing blue light in the distance. It was so eerie to see only that thing. As I drove on the top of the span of the bridge, the wind felt more like a hundred mph. In fact when the officer met me at the wrecker, he told me to hurry because the top wind speed at the bridge's highest point was enough t make the county close this till further notice.

Here is another sorrowful part of my job, which I would like to share with you. The reason I'm doing this is to save loves and maybe change yours. One night I received a call to respond to an accident at the duck pond, which is a man made pond in the city of North Charleston, SC. And when I got there, there were a hundred police cars in the area, and when I got closer I noticed another car in the duck pond. I said, "Ain't this great?" Because I knew who had to go for a little dip, and it sure wasn't in my Olympic size pool.

I just dreaded going in the water because you never knew what you were getting into. At least it was the warm part of the year, but I think it is always cold no matter when you go in. It turned out that the police were trying to stop a car full of dopers, and they were speeding and naturally they went into the duck pond. Which proves a point by now, and as I pulled the car out of the water, there were 4 corpses in it. Let's say this, the care was full of blood, and the smell was bad, a swamp kind of smell. And yes I thought I could smell the blood that was thick and all over the inside of the car. Here is a sticking point that I hope stays with you. The mosquitoes were in the car by the thousands. When I came back to the station, the mosquitoes never left the inside of the car because of their attraction to the blood. It just shows you that alcohol and speed don't mix.

Here is another one, which kind of ended in a happy ending. On a Saturday night this person went out to tone of these clubs and ended up, you guessed it, drunk. Sure enough, he sped right in front of the station after making a U-turn, in which most states is illegal. In fact, he almost collided with another car. The car had to swerve to miss the other auto. In fact, he almost collided with another car. The car had to swerve to miss the other auto. In

GLENN DAVIS | 🐾

fact, he sharply turned the steering wheel to the right, and when he did, the right wheel caught the curb and it flipped the car over six times according to the police report. But guess what, he must have been right with God, because after he rolled the driver's side was up and he had enough sense to climb out of the car. He tried to run before the police and told them about the car, and it sounded awful. I was already in my wrecker and at the scene, and the police asked me how I got there so fast. I told them, "With the way that poor fellow was driving. I figured he wouldn't make it. So I had a feeling it would be right about here as well." And sure enough, I was right, and the boss reaped the reward, some extra money so he could pay off that mortgage rate he had going on his expensive house.

I hope that I can persuade you people not to drink alcohol or to do it with a little common sense. That is, not to drink and drive. I can tell you a couple of stories that would put a pale look on your face because it did me. I hope that I can convince you to be careful about your recreational drinking. Sure, maybe these establishments make money, but I hope that maybe they pay attention to the news about the deaths that occur on the highways each year. I hope that you are ready to hear these stories, and I hope that it will change your mind. However, you are all mature adults, and you will probably make up your own mind and do what ever you want to do.

On a Saturday night I received a call from the County Police about an accident that I had to pick up on Rivers Avenue. It involved a tractor-trailer and an auto. So I had to go through the usual procedure, and pretty soon, I was on the road to the accident so that I could clear the road for other people. As I got there I noticed that there was only a trailer parked in the parking lot, for some unknown reason to fix a tire on his tractor. It was a warm night during the spring, and as it turned out he had a little fun at one of the nearby watering holes. As it turned out, he was driving DUI, and on the way home from parting from the bar, he decided to put on the accelerator to see how fast he could make it home without stopping. Sure enough, he didn't make it, but not only that, you could say it was a mess. He made a wrong turn into the parking lot, and as long as I live I will not forget the experience of seeing my first dead body like that. What happened was after he made a wrong turn, the car was going so fast he didn't have enough reaction time and so his car went underneath the trailer with the top down. When I got there, it looked bad enough with the blood all over the sidewalk and people had to step all over the blood. I proceeded to take the chains and hook it up, and when I did, to my surprise, as I pulled the car out I noticed there was a body all right, but there was no head attached on it.

And another thing, as the car slowly came from under, I noticed that there was a head on the seat next to the body. I don't know if the wind did it or the force of the wrecker pulling the car from under the vehicle, but as I cleared the car the head turned over, and there were his eyes, those eyes. I would never ever forget those eyes as they were opened, and you could see the shocked expression of his face. And sure enough, I could imagine how scared he must've been when all of a sudden this shape appeared out of the darkness and he had no time to do anything.

If that doesn't scare you straight, then here's another scary story to consider. One night, two women decided that they would go out for a few drinks. Little did they know, it would be their last. Here is how it went down. The two women wanted to go out to one of those single bars and try to get matched up with one of those single guys. At the time, I was single myself, but I didn't want to meet them in this way. As they were traveling down the road, at the same time a train crossing signal went off and the arm that blocked people from crossing the track came down as well. Being intoxicated, the women went over the tracks, but at the same time they were running out of gas and as the car slowly came to a halt in the middle of the tracks, the train was coming down to their deaths. If they weren't drinking, speeding towards them, they didn't have a chance. The train rolled the poor car a few hundred yards down the track. And when I went to try to clean up as much of the wreck that I could, I came upon a very attractive looking leg, but it wasn't attached to a body. In fact there were body parts all over the tracks. It would be my job to clear the tracks, and as I picked up the pieces of the car, I noticed pieces of body parts everywhere. I became sick after I got back from the scene. But the worst thing was seeing a headless corpse, and every time that I would go to bed, I would wake up in a cold sweat, and I would sometimes yell out a powerful scream that could wake up the dead.

I was driving on the road one Saturday, paying bills. It was a beautiful summer day; it was very warm and humid as I ventured forth that day. It happened in the afternoon, around lunchtime. All of a sudden, everything went blank. I couldn't see anything at one time. It was pitch black. I started to panic a little bit, but as I started to calm down, I noticed that I had the faith in God to park this car safely and that I would be able somehow to make it home. I slowed the engine down, and with the help of Jesus himself, I was able to find the right road to turn on.

As I sat there for a little while, I noticed that I was blind. The thought of being this way for good haunted me. But as I sat there, in my blue 1950 Ford Maverick, I sure as hell was not taking in the sights in a new town. I was trying to make it home. The first thing that came to mind was to blow the horn and maybe somehow someone would listen and come to the rescue. But somehow, I knew that it was not going to happen that way; I was in a bad section of town.

The only thing I could do was hope that I wouldn't be robbed and hope that my eyesight would come back enough so that I could make it home.

Finally, my vision cleared up enough so that I could make it home, but I know it would be slow going because my vision came back but only to the point of peripheral vision. Not only that, it was out of focus, and my judgment of doing highway driving was minimal. I prayed hard that I would make it home without getting killed. So there I was, creeping along, while the other people behind them were blowing their horns and cursing me out without any provocation on my part. I lifted my hands up as to say what can I do? I was helpless as I could be.

As I finally made it home, using my fine gift of memory, I found my way to the front door, not being accustomed to unlocking the door. I finally made it to the front door and yelled out to my dad. Banging on the door at the same time and said, "Help me!" As Dad rushed to my side, he asked me, "Are you all right, son?" I calmly told my dad that I lost my eyesight and that I needed to go see the doctor right away." My dad told me, that I needed to go see the doctor right away." My dad told me, "Well, the doctor's office is closed right now until Monday morning, and when the day comes you will see him then, but for right now the best thing for you to do is go to bed."

After calming down, I realized that it would be pointless for me to go on and make a fool of myself, crying and carrying on when it was possible that the Lord Jesus had other plans for me, and it would be a lot better on me if I just laid back and see what plans that the Lord had in store for me.

Monday morning came, and we got into the car and went to the MUSC Storm Eye Institute, where they specialize in the loss of vision. The doctor walked into the office and asked me how I was. I looked at him and said, "Well, I'm here to see you, Doc. I must not be doing so hot." The doc laughed and said, "Someone is grouchy today?" And as I was sitting there in the office chair, I was thinking to myself, "Yeah, if you lost your sight or most of it, I guess you would be cool as a cucumber."

As the doctor went through the procedure of examining my eyes, he kept saying 'Mamma." As I looked at him, guessing by the direction of his voice, I said "Doc, it makes me nervous when you say that." "I have good reason. Do you know what diabetes stands for?" I looked at him and said, "No, sir. I don't." "I think what the problem is that your blood sugar level is high which is impairing your vision, or the eye is hemorrhaging. That means that the blood vessels in the back of your eye are multiplying so fast and breaking and that is what is causing you to bleed in the back of your retina. That, in turn, will cause you to lose your sight."

I said to the doc, "That's just great, Doc. Is there anything else that you need to tell me?" The doc, who looked sympathetic, said, "The only thing we can do is to run some tests on you and see how high your blood sugar or anything else for that matter is." The doctor, who must have noticed the worried look on my face, said, "Don't worry, all this is a simple blood test, which would tell us how high your sugar reading is." I nodded my head in agreement. "That this is the best thing to do."

"The nurse will be here in a few minutes to take a sample of your blood, and we will go from there. Okay?" I shook my head yes, and he patted me on the shoulder and said, "Again, I won't to tell you how brave you are and that everything will be all right." As I sat waiting, the nurse came in with a smile on her face, and she took rubbing alcohol and rubbed, where she was going to put the needle into my arm. I braced as she quickly did it. As she did it, she looked at me with a smile and said, "That didn't hurt a bit now, did it?" I told her, "If you were to change places with me and if I asked you that, what would you tell me sitting here?" She did not say anything. She walked away, as if to tell me that it wouldn't feel good either.

As the minutes ticked away into an hour, the doctor and the nurse finally walked in with the good news that they hoped to find, and the fact of the matter was that it was diabetes that was causing me to lose my sight. It seems the disease causes a lot of problems when you gain weight. The only thing they could do at the time to bring the numbers down was to prescribe insulin. And back in the old days, that was injected by the needle.

And as time progressed, I was recommended to an organization known as the commission for the blind, which helps people who have lost their sight and trains them for jobs, adjustment, and mobility. They teach you Braille and other things that will assist the blind to cope with everyday life. When I became used to mobility, I noticed that certain people used a dog to get around, and curious as I was, I started to ask questions about owning a dog such as theirs. The first thing that would come out of their mouths was that the animal they use to get around is called a guide dog, meaning it goes anywhere you go, like for instance, any government building, hospital, library, store, or any place a man or woman can go. I became more interested in this, so I called the Southeastern guide dog school for the blind, and they showed me how to go about doing the paper work to obtain a guide dog. It seemed reasonably fast to obtain the information about when the next class would be too.

The next thing I knew, I was at the guide dog school waiting to get a dog. The first couple of days that I was there was mostly to get accustomed to the school, because when you are in the school with a dog, the dog is off duty and will not guide you when it is off duty. The next step is for the trainer to get you equipped with a harness and the way that they do that is to measure your pull by walking with your harness. The next day, you finally be able to receive your companion for the rest of your life. There is a lot of responsibility in having a guide dog. This should be the rule with any dog, having the responsibility of taking care of it.

During the last couple of weeks of training, I noticed that I had some bad coughing going on. Also, I had some bad wheezing in my chest. I told one of the trainers about it, and she noticed that the coughing was getting worse. I told her that for the past few days, I wasn't telling anyone because I love my dog, and I didn't want anything to interrupt training. She understood my plight and told me that if for anytime during the training that I needed to go to the hospital that I shouldn't hesitate to call her and tell her. I agreed, but in my mind, I was afraid that if I told them, they would take Bailey away from me. I didn't want that to happen at any cost, so I ventured forth in my training, and sure enough, it came to graduation day. The only ceremony was signing the paper work stating that it is your dog. I was so thrilled when that day finally happened, but the cough lingered on. I made up my mind that evening as I breathed in and all liquid came up in my chest.

I told the trainer, "Look, I'm on fixed income, but I'm here to tell you that I'm not able to afford any kind of medical bill right now because I had a wife and we both were living on a fixed income." But the trainer told me not to worry about it and that I could make little payments until it was paid off. I agreed only because I know I had the training done, and now I wanted to get better so that I could rest.

We drove to the hospital the next morning, and I entered the hospital with one of the trainers who sat with me and made sure I was taken in all right. They had always assured me that everything was all right and that they were proud of me and that I would not give up. The doctor came in an after the tests were done, the doctor told me that it was a miracle that I lasted long as I had. He told me, "Sir, you have to go in the hospital now. I'm here to tell you that you have bronchitis, pneumonia."

There are so many guide dog owners that give up their dog for many reasons. They cannot afford it, food or vet bills, or the rejection of society when it concerns the use of a guide dog in their building. There are a lot of misconceptions about guide dogs, such as the mess that they leave behind. If you take your dog out that morning after chow, nine times out of ten, the dog will not mess anywhere till the afternoon. Guide dogs are potty trained and would not mess in a building or in your home or another person's home. This seems to be the biggest concern with most people. Secondly, most people always have the wrong impression that it is a dog. Wrong: it is a guide dog, and this should be made clear by the harness that they wear. The dogs are also used for other purposes for people with other disabilities.

As I went through training, I learned a lot. The second week of training is usually called puppy trainer's raiser's week. This is a week in which puppy raisers came down to see if their hard work in raising them from a puppy would pay off.

The fourth week, the dogs go through a rigorous obstacle course with you. You also, go through training as well as residential training. You have to remember that each dog has a personality all their own and their own uniqueness. I have to chuckle when I notice the things that my guide dog goes through. For instance, at the school, she has a time with a goose named Gertrude. She doesn't like any of the dogs that come through. In fact, she has nipped my dog several times during my training.

During the weeks of being in the hospital I was thinking about my wife and what she must be going through. Meanwhile back home, my wife was contacted by the school and apprised her of my condition. Needles to say, when they told her not to worry, that was an understatement. She wanted to be with me, but at the time, she knew that we couldn't afford it. But during the time I was in the hospital, and as I lay there with the IV pouring into my arm, I saw Jesus as plain as day, looking me straight in the face shaking his head as if to say. "You are going to be back home with your wife, and that I have other plans for you." As I came back into life, I have done exactly that. I have lived by the good book and when I came back home, I received that big hug from my wife, who was with a friend to help wait for my safe return into her arms. And the best thing of all was seeing my guide dog hopping on her and giving her a big kiss. It was worth the reward, and ever since then, my special companion and I have been together for five years now.

And let me tell you this. One day while working her in the mall, not only did my dog stop me from falling down the stairs, she stopped my wife's friend and my wife from falling sown the same stairs.

Not only that, my guide dog, who I'm so proud of till this day, has also saved a friend of ours from colliding into a bathroom wall. I look back on this and smile for I have accomplished a lot. The best advice I have for a blind person out there is never be afraid to ask. And I also thank God because I could not do this without him. My guide dog is the best, and with her it's like having vision through God's eyes.

CPSIA information can be obtained at www.ICGtesting.com
Printed in the USA
BVOW04s0844220115

384483BV00007B/17/P